PREACHER'S TALE

Josiah Brooks

Reed Light Books

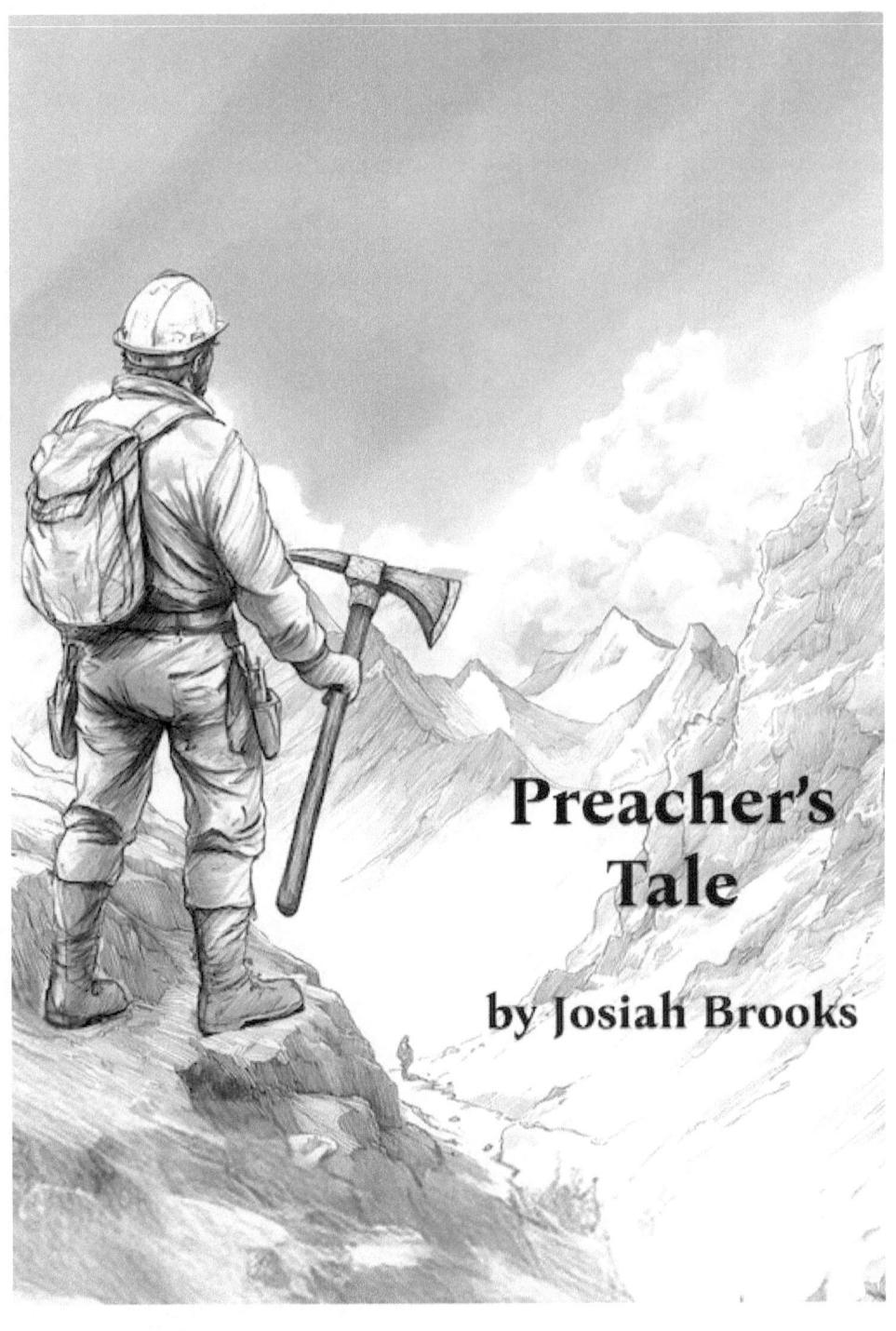

Preacher's Tale

by Josiah Brooks

Preacher's Tale

By Josiah Brooks
© 2025

For all the miners in the mountain;
Those who labor long and dig deep.

Neither you nor your toil are forgotten.
You are seen and held by Him who never sleeps.

CONTENTS

CHAPTER 1: INTO THE MINE I GO!

Preacher roused himself; his orders had come in once again: "All-hands meeting; 6 days. 10 o'clock, sharp!" *That means 8AM for me.*

He'd just walked out of an all-hands meeting yesterday, now Preacher had to prepare for another one in six days! This part of the job was tough!

So, into the mines he would go again. Would Foreman be there tomorrow? He didn't know. Would he find another treasure? He didn't know.

All Preacher knew was that it was his job to make the dig, bring back some of the treasure he'd found, and present it at the all-hands meeting. Today, he was too tired from yesterday's meeting. So, he'd begin tomorrow.

Wait, Preacher thought.
I need to send my note to Foreman know I'm coming. I'll send the note ahead - and ask him to meet me. Another week, another note!

So, he wrote:

Attention: Foreman,

Good afternoon, Sir. Thank you for your assistance with last week's meeting. Your notes and attendance were helpful, as always.

I've been informed that this week will bring another meeting where I will present. I kindly request your assistance in the mines. Please direct my attention to the most fruitful digs. You know this mountain. Your assistance will significantly advance my work.

Sincerely,

Preacher

Sounds good enough. Preacher thought. *I hope Foreman isn't too busy this week. He can be helpful in a pinch.*

The next morning, Preacher followed his normal routine. He woke up and imagined a route to where he thought the mines would be most productive. Over coffee, he tapped his pen on his head as he remembered how last week, the route he planned had little to do with the route he needed in the end. Still, scribbling out a map, he even made some notes for his presentation.

"That should be good. This should be an easy presentation on Sunday! The gold I struck last week was beautiful! I'm sure I'll find more of the same this week." He smiled. "Maybe I can show Foreman that I'm pretty competent on my own!"

Little did Preacher know how wrong he was.

As he walked, Preacher had some pep in his step. "I've gotten pretty good at these presentations! I think I can pretty much write the script now, even without mining!" He smiled to himself and waved to Foreman - who looked up as Preacher passed the mobile office.

"I've got this one!" Preacher said. Preacher noticed a slight fade to the smile on Foreman's face. Not in anger, just...was that disappointment? Still, Preacher closed the door of the elevator and pushed the arrow labeled "Down."

Surely, it will make Foreman happy to see me improving. I'll show him I've got what it takes to get ahead in this business!

Preacher sang:

> *Into the mine, I go!*
> *Oh, into the mine, I go!*
> *Where it leads, I'll follow*
> *It's both full and hollow!*
> *Oh, into the mine, I go!*

"I never understood that," Preacher thought. "How could the mine be full and hollow? What a weird song we miners sing."

As the elevator clunked along, Preacher flicked on his helmet light and lit up his map. "That's where I'm going! Next five feet along last week's path. There was gold there last week. There will be gold again this week! That's how it works. Gold leads to gold!"

The elevator click-clacked along. Its cables and bolts

whined and shook the deeper he got.

Preacher looked up and saw the blue sky at the top of the shaft he'd traveled down. The light seemed to turn white as he sank lower, descending through the layers he'd carved week after week.

"Oh...into....the.....mine....I go..." Preacher slowly hummed the line again. Everywhere his head turned, the rock seemed to ignite in a radiant glow. How much of the glow was from the minerals in the tunnel? How much was from the lamp he wore? Preacher didn't know. Still, he smiled as he remembered each cavern.

There's the garnet line! Garnet Gallery. Sheesh, the granite really tore my axe to shreds, but I'll never forget how happy I was to find garnet in the midst of it! Then, there were twenty new miners who came on board after the presentation of the garnets! Twenty!

The elevator sank deeper.

"Oh, Jade Junction!" Preacher said aloud even though there was no one else around. Feeling a bit silly, he only thought to himself as he smiled:
I never knew there was jade here! The jade presentation wasn't easy, but thirty miners signed on immediately afterwards! Then, five more came later because they heard about the jade from the others in the crowd!

The elevator sank deeper.

"Uggh" Preacher said it with disgust. *I broke four axes in that cave. I broke four axes and ruined three more! And all for what? Limestone Landing. Crummy old, boring old, limestone. I have no earthly idea why those ten new investors signed on after that presentation. Who cares about limestone?!*

Preacher descended into the mountain. Each layer represented time he'd spent mining. Each was met with fond or foul memories of subsequent presentations he'd made. He'd dig and dig. He'd find something new. He'd bring it up on the elevator. Then, each week Preacher would bring a picture of his quarry with him and he'd make his best pitch to a listening crowd of anywhere from ten to a few hundred listeners in the auditorium. Some would lean in, some would smile as he spoke. Others would take notes on his presentation. Sometimes, Preacher felt like his presentations were world class and he swelled with joy as he'd share about each rock, gem, or mineral. In those times, Preacher was thrilled that the people would write feverishly on their notepads as he glowed about what he'd brought to share. Other times, Preacher had to try his best to hold their attention. Like the limestone he brought. Even Preacher wasn't sure about the appeal of limestone, so he was not surprised when people seemed to be confused as he spoke. Still, on the whole, Preacher hoped he could inspire the people to mine for themselves.

Some did. Most didn't.

Preacher was never quite sure why those came to the presentations.

Why do they even come? They just sit there through these presentations. Do they just like rocks or what? Or maybe it's that they like hearing us talk about rocks but don't really have any interest in them personally.

"I don't know," he'd say to his fellow miners, "Maybe they're looking for a job, so they sit in and hope Foreman will like it that they came."

Preacher furrowed his brow as he thought about it. He passed Turquoise Trail, Emerald Excavation, Ruby Rift. Then, Lapis Ledge, Beryl Bench, Fluorite Field.

It's kind of weird, I guess. Sometimes I'm not really sure just what it is that I'm doing here. Do these presentations really make a difference? I mean, I've done hundreds through the years, but only average about five or ten new hires per presentation! Those aren't great metrics!

Preacher flipped the catch as he came to last week's dig. *Gold Gateway!* The elevator rumbled to a stop.

As he fumbled with the door, Preacher started to feel some excitement.

I can't believe I finally struck gold last week! Mining 101 says there should be more gold where I found it last week! I can't wait to get digging again!

Preacher hopped out of the elevator with a bounce in his step. *Gold, gold, here I come!*

With a flick of his wrist, Preacher threw the elevator door closed. The "Clang!" reverberated throughout the cavern.

Something in the elevator caught Preacher's eye as he turned to face last week's cavern.

The green "UP" button was on!

"Oh no!" Preacher's reaction was too slow and too late. The elevator sprang to life. The door latched, the wires caught and somewhere far above, Preacher knew the wheels were turning again, to take the elevator back up.

He looked, but Preacher was far too deep, now, for his light to reach the top or for his eyes to see the top of the mine shaft.

All he could do was stare up in disbelief.

CHAPTER 2: THE ROLE OF LAST WEEK'S PROFIT

Preacher felt around his tool belt and his head lamp. A shudder of cold cave air shook him.

"Wait." He said aloud. "I've trained for this. Trust the process. Trust the process. Trust the process. What are the four

P's?"

"Power. Plan. Purpose and...Pickaxe!" He nodded his head to punctuate each word, then shook his axe in the air.

"Power: Yep," He patted his vest where the fresh batteries were packed each morning. "I have power."

"Plan: Check!" Preacher took out his map and flicked his head lamp down as he'd done so many hundreds of times. The snap landed the light beam right on the map in his left hand. "I've got my plan! This map is my plan and I'm here in the Gold Gateway!"

"Purpose: Yes." Preacher looked up into the mineshaft, again. He swallowed hard as he noticed the elevator was barely visible as it rose. "Yes. I...I have my purpose. The all-hands meeting is in 5 days and I need to get some treasure to share with everyone there. Purpose: Check!"

"And...Pickaxe: Yup. That's the easy one." He swiveled the pickaxe in his hand. Years of lifting, carrying, and swinging had solidified Preacher's strength to allow this impressive feat. He spun the twenty-pound pickaxe like it was smooth and light as a ball peen hammer. "Got it!" He caught the spinning pickaxe so the handle aligned perfectly and the sharp end faced away from him. He loved to do that during the presentations to wow the crowd. He smiled as he said it again, "Power, plan, purpose, pickaxe."

The rehearsed words brought some comfort to Preacher. He knew what he was doing. Still, he couldn't stop himself from thinking other, less comforting thoughts.

Elevator. *No, I don't have the elevator schedule. I don't know how long it will take for someone else to come down here. Who checks on a miner in his own mine?*

Water. Preacher swallowed involuntarily. *I have some for a while. Will it be enough?*

Oxygen. Preacher breathed in deeply. *Is there enough down here? What will I do if I run out? What can I do?*

Feeling a bit sad, Preacher turned angry and started to berate himself.

Foolish! So foolish! What were you thinking? You weren't thinking! It was the gold, wasn't it? You got so caught up in dreaming about the gold that you sent the elevator back up the tube!

Wait, come on. Snap out of it. Power, plan, purpose, pickaxe. Then, he said it aloud: "Power, plan, purpose, pickaxe."

Preacher straightened up and gathered his supplies.

Well, you're here. You might as well get to work! You do still have that presentation in 5 days, after all! Wait, no. It's four now!

The reminder provided the motivation Preacher needed. *Why did I take off yesterday? Now I have even less time!*

He gathered himself and his supplies, then started walking.

Ahh, here we are!

Preacher grinned as he saw last week's tunnel and he walked to the farthest point he'd carved.

Then, Preacher started the tested and proven method he'd learned so many years before:

See the rock, know the rock, get the rock, use the rock.

Preacher had been taught how to handle the mountain. "If you follow this method, you can always make the mountain useful," his teacher had told him. "It will help you dig, and help you give your presentations. Honestly, you could even structure your presentations around this too! See the rock, know the rock, get the rock, use the rock. Then, you can help others."

He remembered his teacher fondly. "If only he could see

me now! All the caverns I've cut. All the rock I've seen, known, gotten out, and used! I have jade fixtures all over my house. I have emerald in my walls at home, and garnets the size of my head in my office!"

"Ok." He said, setting his kit down. "I see you!" His eyes did shine a bit as Preacher looked at the wall. Sure enough, there was the gold! It glimmered, like tiny lights when it reflected the beam from his headlamp.

Nothing glimmers like gold!

Preacher looked at the wall closely, running his hands over the rock. His fingers, rough with wear, found the surface, hard and jagged. There were points and picks in the wall. Preacher read the rock like a Braille reader nearing the end of an epic saga. Hungrily, his touch devoured each square inch without leaving a mark. His breathing slowed. His eyes closed. The beauty in the mine was not seen with eyes. Not by the miner, at least. It was felt. He spread his fingers wide as he moved them. He pressed his palms against the surface. More contact was definitely best. Preacher inhaled slowly.

"I love being a miner." Preacher whispered it.

This rock wasn't cold, it was just the right amount of heat.

He traced the chipped surface where he had last thrown his axe before going back up, last week.

"Here it is."

Shining his light on the wall, Preacher's eyes found the place he'd felt.

"I see you." He said.

Then, his face moving from ardor to intensity in one moment, habit took over. He scanned the surface quickly. Preacher lightly patted the rock two times and straightened his back.

"I know you." He said.

He found his spot. Preacher placed one boot right up against the wall, took a step back and two side-steps to the left. With a slow stride, he turned, more gliding than shuffling. Without looking, Preacher tossed aside his pack and lifted the axe to his shoulder.

"I'm coming for you." He said.

With his body facing 90 degrees from the wall, Preacher turned his head to look at it.

"From the mountain…"

Effortlessly, he shifted his weight and repositioned his feet.

"To the miner!"

His feet knew where to go. The boots he wore dug into the powdery mix, finding firm purchase underfoot, as he turned. The axe moved in the air. His eyes and the hardened steel point facing the same direction, up and away from the wall. His torso twisted away as he inhaled.

Graceful like petals unfolding for the dew of morning; powerful like a Joshua tree unraveling for its maker, Preacher unwound his body. The power shifting from his legs to his chest, down his arms, through his hands, Preacher thrilled the axe. In one moment, he gave the axe its meaning and purpose as it hurled through the crisp air, splitting the subterranean night and biting into the ore in front of Preacher.

No sparks flew from the union but the sound was deafening and beautiful.

It crackled and erupted through the cavern, echoing deeper with each reverberation.

"Sing to me." Preacher called into the tunnel. He smiled as he turned back to the rock.

There was a rumbling, a shifting, and Preacher's mouth turned to a grin and his eyes grew wide.

CHAPTER 3: CHASING GOLD, FINDING METTLE

Memories of his last time in this Golden Gateway began to ignite in Preacher's thoughts. Faster than conscious thought, mental images of hands holding the golden chunks filled him. Images of himself smiling, teased his imagination; it was the smile he must have had as he loaded rock after rock, chunk after chunk of shining gold into the mine cart. Then:

What an odd thing to think about!

Preacher remembered the sound of the metal cart wheels as they creak-creaked under the strain of so much gold in the cart. He remembered how happy he was to make the cart strain in that way. "This is what you're here for! If you break under this strain, I'll just grab another cart!" He had said, last week.

Then, in the blink of an eye, Preacher pictured himself sharing at the all-hands meeting. He remembered himself, holding that chunk of gold high up in the air in front of everyone in the room! "Look! There is gold to be had! Foreman's mines are full of gold! I've seen it! I have it! You can have it too! Join up and mine with me! The life of a miner is good. So, so good. Follow me! I'll help you mine for yourselves!"

The eyes of every person in the room were trained on Preacher and he loved it. That picture lingered in his imagination: Preacher, in his meeting clothes, smiling broadly and holding up the gold for the crowd to see - and all their eyes wide and round like pearls with sapphires in the centers.

His breathing had become shallow and Preacher was quivering with anticipation.

Then, Preacher heard the noise he was waiting for. A four foot high, three foot wide, 5 inch thick slab fell away from the surface; released by his mighty heave - the depth and power of his strike. This was less an explosion and more a yielding, as the great rock slumped to the ground.

Eagerly, Preacher directed his light to where it had fallen.

Then, he began the phrase he used each time he revealed a new treasure in the mine:

"I have seen. I have known. I have struck. I've gotten, gol—"

Preacher heaved, with one end on the stone floor, he turned over the mighty slab like he was opening the lid to a treasure chest. But before he could finish his little rhyme, he was shocked to find no gleam of yellow reflecting back to him.

He leaned in closer. Not trusting his eyes, Preacher ran his hands across the surface. He brushed away the non-existent layer of dust, hoping a glimmer would be revealed. It was clear and the clarity was the pain.

"No gold."

Preacher stood up. His eyes traced the path of the golden vein he'd found last week. The vein he'd tapped. The vein he'd retrieved with many trips to the surface in an elevator full of treasure. Preacher had left only the faint trail he attempted to uncover today.

He retraced his steps. Over and over, Preacher turned the slab this way and that. Sure enough, he saw only the faint outline of gold left over to show him where to strike. Last week, it was as if the very blood of the mountain coursed through these veins and the life was pure gold. The jagged radiance followed the pattern of every gold line he'd ever seen. And every other line following this pattern, dove into the rock - deeper and wider, not diminishing in less than six inches of rock.

I know.

Preacher stood up and took a deep breath. He smiled to himself with a certainty he was starting to question.

He restarted his habitual approach. Preacher knew what he was doing. Years of treasure hunting and work in the mines had produced some habits he now clung to.

"I see you." He furrowed his brow, moving his face to intensity, yet again. He scanned the newly exposed and all dark surface. Preacher patted the rock, his face showing that he was more coaxing than appreciating the rock. "I…know you?" He said.

Do I? He thought.

Preacher found his spot. He placed a boot against the wall, took a step back and those same two side-steps to the left. He turned with unsure shuffling steps. Preacher lifted the axe to his shoulder. "I'm…coming…for you." Preacher said.

With his body facing 90 degrees from the wall, Preacher turned his head to look at it. "From…the mountain…" With a care, Preacher shifted his weight and repositioned his feet. "To the miner!"

One foot came up as the other dug into the sand underfoot. The axe moved in the air, his eyes and the hardened steel point both seemed unsure of what would happen next. His torso twisted away as he took a quick gulp of air.

He powered through. Preacher tightened every muscle and spun his body into the swing. Trained, powerful arms pushed the axe through the arc towards the wall. The axe whistled and crashed in on the rock.

Again, there were no sparks and the sound was different. Instead of the ringing beauty of the steel's dance with the rock, this time, the steel just seemed to bash the raw face.

"*Thwank!*" The axe and rock screamed together.

"Sing for me!" Preacher yelled more than called into the tunnel. He turned back to the rock.

This time, a six inch by twelve inch sheet fell off the wall and broke into pieces on the ground. Preacher quickly inspected the pile.

"No!" He defied the rock for its dark rebellion against his hopes.

No glimmer. No gold.

"But, last week!" Preacher said aloud.

He huffed and stood up. "I am a miner!"

Preacher repeated the process.

He kicked his boot to the wall. He backed up one step and took two steps left! He addressed the rock! He turned! He swung! He crashed the rock!

Crumbles fell.

He inspected the pile. Nothing of worth. Again!

Preacher stood up! Kicked the wall! One step back! Two steps left! Address! Turn! Swing! Crash!

Crumbles. Inspect. Nothing.

Again!

Preacher went on for hours.

"I have seen. I have known. I have gotten…Nothing!"

Stand. Kick! Step! Step, step! Turn, swing! Crash! Crumble. Inspect!

Preacher could barely swing the axe any more.

"What have I seen?" Preacher looked at the pile around him. It was all dark. "What is this?!" He shouted. "What was last week? Was that even gold?"

"What am I doing here? Aaaagghh!"

Preacher threw down his axe and heaved. As he wiped his brow with a dusty hand, his gasps for air filled the cave with a sound oddly different from that one created by the axe-assaults on the mountain.

He reached to take his hard hat off and it slipped when he

pulled it. His sweaty brow had drenched the rim and his aching hands were so tired and clumsy that the hat could have been taken from him on a wish.

The hard hat slipped. Lunging and grabbing at it desperately, Preacher missed, and punched it farther away. It flew a few feet and slid on the hard ground. Then, the thing he least expected happened.

The light on his headlamp flickered and went out.

"No." Preacher gasped. His mouth and eyes were wide open in a shock of horror.

His arms were still reaching for the hat when the light went out.

Suddenly, everything was completely still.

"No...no....no!" Preacher wailed. He pulled his hands into fists, using the dark as cover for this display of emotion.

The echo moaned back at him from far away in the cavern. He whipped his head around, gazing in a fruitless search of the dark. He withdrew his arms, hugging himself for comfort.

Preacher slowly and subconsciously moved into a crouch. Making himself small, Preacher pulled in his arms; hovering over his legs, he had to steady himself from this unusual position. His knuckles were sore from where he'd hit the hat. Against his own wishes to be calm, Preacher's mind raced from the haunting scene and his own uncertainty.

Then, in a way he least expected and least wanted to think - the words came back to Preacher:

> *Where it leads, I'll follow*
> *It's both full and hollow!*
> *Oh, into the mine, I go!*

"Not hollow! Not now!"

Far away, there was a "Blupp."

Preacher spun to hear it. He shut his eyes and craned his neck the slightest bit. Every bit of his energy was given to listening. Stock still, Preacher kept himself tuned for the smallest sound he might have heard.

But there was no more sound.

He waited longer.

In the blackest dark of the cave without a light or lantern, Preacher finally opened his eyes again. He adjusted his neck and moved his head back to its normal angle. He lowered his shoulders...

I guess I'm hearing things.

"Teetle clup...Blupp." He bolted upright and snapped his neck again, to listen closely.

Are those footsteps?

CHAPTER 4: AN UNEXPECTED VISITOR

Preacher imagined little feet, scurrying across the stony ground. His mental image led from the little feet to little legs and little bodies. He imagined angry little trolls, running through the tunnels. Their angry little faces bounced as they hopped from rock to rock.

As he listened, though, Preacher could only hear his own breathing. With scorn, he shook his head.

How many times have I been in this tunnel, and I'm shaking like a leaf! And what is that thudding? Oh, it's me! It sounds like my heart is beating through my chest!

"Teetle clup...Blupp."

There it is again!

He waited.

"Teetle clup...Blupp." *It's too regular. It must not be footsteps.*

"Hellooooooooo?" Preacher called with fear and hope.

If there's someone there, I want to know.

"Teetle...teetle clup...blupp."

It's water. Of course!

Relief washed over Preacher. He rolled his eyes, embarrassed of himself and the way he'd let his imagination overwhelm him.

"Wauuuuuuuuuuun Wahhhhhhhnnnn" This new sound was so faint and so remote, Preacher could only barely hear it. Like a foghorn on the ocean on a dreary winter morning, he heard the metal loon. Still, if he'd been moving, he'd have missed it - it was so faint. This time, though, there was recognition and not fear.

Well, I know what that is. That's just the work bell, reminding everyone of their shift.

And then, Preacher wept.

He wept for his situation. He wept for his fear. He wept for his job. Preacher wept for his friends up at the top of the mine shaft; and how they were just going about their business without knowing about him. He pictured them hard at work - without caring for him at all.

Does anyone know? I've been gone awhile now. Do they even care? Probably not, everyone else has their own mines to dig. They're too busy to think about me down here. Did anyone see me come today? Did they realize I never came back up? Does anyone miss me? Maybe they just assume I hit another huge load and I'm hauling it up slowly. Ugg, the load; the gold. How could I miss the gold? I hit it right where I left it! Where else would it be? You strike a vein and follow it! And, how could I break my lamp?

When he'd wept for a while, Preacher opened his eyes and strained for light.

Then, he wept some more.

"How could this have happened?" He sobbed.

"I am a miner! This is my job! I dig! How can I fail at digging? Where is the gold? Where is the garnet, now? Where's the jade? The silver? The emerald? Where are the rubies? I'll even take the limestone!"

Yelling the last one, Preacher sobbed even more.

He pictured himself holding limestone, lifting up the grey and white brick as he had during that presentation. He'd tried so hard to make it seem beautiful.

Suddenly, he stopped. "Oh no! The presentation! What will I do?"

Preacher sat up but quickly realized it made no difference in the dark. It actually made him more fearful that he'd sat up without seeing.

How high is the ceiling in here? Did I leave room for myself to stand up? This is silly. Of course I did! I was standing when I broke the lamp.

"What will I share at the all-hands meeting? Will I even make it? I could die down here!"

"But...but really...what difference does it make about the all-hands meeting if I'm dead? I'm down in the mine, with no gold, no light, no axe, no plan. I've got a sore hand, I'm cave blind, the elevator's gone. I can't even move, because I could fall down farther."

"Why did I become a miner in the first place? All the other miners I recruited can't help me now. I'm so lost. They're in their own tunnels. And I'm down here. All al—"

"Not alone."

Preacher froze in place. *What was that?! Where did it come from?* The voice felt like it was in front of him and behind him.

The words caught in his mouth before he could say them, "Heh—" He cleared his throat. "Hello?!"

It was no good, looking around the cave with its devastating absence of anything approaching light, but Preacher did it anyway.

"Who said that?" Preacher wasn't afraid. He was curious.

Where did that voice come from? Was there someone in the cave with him? Had some thief heard about the gold? Was someone trying to steal it?

Well, there's no more gold here! There's nothing to steal!

"Hello?" His voice echoed once again from every corner of every rock wall.

That made him stop calling. The resounding echoes were too much for him and Preacher couldn't think straight when the only sound reverberating was that of his own voice.

Gone were the tinkling sounds of the water. Whether they were absorbed into his own subconscious or Preacher was too focused on the voice he'd heard - he didn't know.

Preacher stayed as still as he could manage.

Where is my axe? I need my axe. Oh, why did I break that light? I'd be able to find my axe if I had my light.

The silence was just about too much for Preacher when he looked up. *What just happened?*

Preacher started to wonder about how he knew he was looking up. He'd been looking all over and in every direction for a long time now, but this was the first time he knew he was looking up.

Why? What changed?

Just then, the cavern filled with light. Preacher tried to look up to the source, but had to cover his eyes quickly!

"Ahhh!" He shouted and recoiled.

Preacher was about to complain, when he heard a distant and familiar sound.

"Ohhhhh!"

The voice rang out from the very top of the tunnel. Still, Preacher could tell it was so smooth, so delightful, so strong.

"Ohhhhh, welcome to my mountain, the hill of my joy.
This is my mountain; for every girl and boy.
Take my hand, and walk with me
Find your rest and then you'll see..."

Preacher could not pull his eyes from the top of the mine shaft; indeed, he didn't want to. The voice of a rich baritone brought colors to his mind's eye and he found his heart was warmed. Tears began to form as his eyes searched, without straining, to see more of the source of the melody.

What? I...I know this song.

As he gazed upward, Preacher looked in wonder. Slowly, each cavern he'd once worked filled with a new brilliance. Warm light and an inviting glow seemed to ignite each wall, shimmer, and then pour out into the next level below. Years of caverns where he'd scraped and dug were being illuminated. But no shadows formed! The light had a fullness such that it created no shade. Instead, it filled cracks and crevices like it was alive, chasing the darkness and leaving new light behind! Light, like the tongues of a vast campfire seemed to undulate like the sun itself was flowing into the tunnel. Wrapped in the rich amber yellows were blankets of bold orange and reds, blowing like linens in the summer breeze on a line. Weaving in and out of the photopic river were threads of sapphire, shimmering as they peeked in and out. Shining, translucent greens and rich violets bubbled up in a cadence that seemed, at once, wild and chaotic, yet peaceful and rhythmic.

Preacher's mind swam as his head moved in a lazy dance, tilting and bending. He knew the song, but not the words. *How is that possible? This song is in me; it's part of me. Still, I don't know how the words go.*

He listened more.

Without knowing the words, though - I know how they should sound. The words echo in my soul like a long-lost friend. There's a place for them inside of me and I want to hear them more.

Soon, his body followed his head. Preacher realized that he, too, was slowly swaying in gentle accord with the orchestra of color and harmony.

"This is my mountain, where strain and stress are eased
Join me at the mountain; with you I'm deeply pleased.
I have built and I have made

The rocks and gems of every cave...."

Preacher had walked to the edge of the tunnel and only then did he realize the elevator was silhouetted against the light.

It's coming from the top. He thought. *It's moving with the light! The elevator is coming down with the light!*

The song continued as Preacher watched.

I...I feel afraid. Preacher realized as he listened. Still, he couldn't bring himself to stop staring.

Whether it was hours or moments; seconds, or the blink of an eye, Preacher didn't know. Suddenly, though, he noticed the elevator was only one floor away.

Preacher became frantic. He patted his chest where the extra batteries for his lamp were stored. He reached for his axe but remembered, again, it had been thrown aside in frustration. He flushed with shame as he remembered his failure at the wall and the way he crumbled under the pressure. Wanting to play the man, Preacher reached for his hard hat the way he always did. His left hand reached for the brim as his right hand reached for the lamp. He wanted to turn it off, now that the light and song were so close. But his hands found no brim and no lamp. Only the cool moist hair and his forehead received his reaching hands. He put his hands on his forehead with a sigh: *My hat, I remember.*

"Delight in my mountain, there's plenty here to do,
Come work in my mountain, there's purpose for you, too!
Soil, earth, and gems await
Like lapis, topaz, and agate!"

Preacher held a hand up to shield his eyes. The light was flowing from the elevator!

Preacher squinted and moved his head around to see what was happening. He could barely see. Every time Preacher tried to see, the light was too bright for him. Then, he'd hide his eyes again. When he hid his eyes, he'd move his hand and try again to see. All he could see, though, was the overflowing waves of light. It streamed from the elevator as he tried to watch where it would go.

Then, it stopped. The elevator silently came to rest at the level where Preacher stood, only a dozen feet away.

Suddenly, his mind raced. Preacher pictured himself smiling and running hard through a field.

Why was I running so hard?

He thought of a warm, sunny day, on a weekend in June. His mind whirled with thoughts of laughter and memories of tiny hands, picking blackberries. He laughed at himself in the memory as he thought of eating them and wiping his hands on his shirt.

Then, he remembered pouring fresh sweet cream over the blackberries and eating them with a spoon. He remembered his mother, smiling at him as he grinned up at her with blackberry juice between his teeth.

That smile. I remember that smile. I...I remember this.

Then, Preacher realized he could see again. The person on the elevator was becoming clear.

Is....Is that...Wait.

CHAPTER 5: NEVER ALONE

"Oh! Foreman! Foreman! I'm so glad to see you! Thank you for coming down! Whoa! Can you believe this light?! Where is all this coming from?! What did you put on the elevator? Some new feature? Some new lamp system? Whoa! I've never seen anything like that. I mean, I've seen things that—"

"Hello, Ephraim."

Preacher had been rambling. The questions, the comments, the words had fallen out of him. Now, he slowed.

"I....I...I've seen...things...that..."

That voice.

"Ephraim."
There it is again!

Suddenly, Preacher's mind went to another day. He was running again! Down the grassy hill where he'd skinned his knee when he was eight; it was so bad! One small trip and he'd tumbled down from next to the hickory tree to the bottom, by the jumping rock! But he didn't care about his knee! This time, he was fearless, running and smiling again. Then, he had stopped and taken off his shoes.

I know! I know what happened next!

In his mind's eye, Preacher saw himself taking off his shoes and throwing them aside. Then, he ran so fast and so hard across the grass, across the little pond's pier, and he jumped! Into the air he went, with his arms held out as far as they could reach and his fingers spread like he could fling them right off his hands! The smile he wore then was as big as anyone could ever smile! Then, he hit the pond with a huge "SPLASH!"

Preacher blinked and saw that Foreman was smiling. Preacher quickly regained his composure.

"Foreman! Whoa! You won't believe the timing! I'm so glad you came down here today! I've been stuck down here for a while! And just now, I've been having the strangest things happen to me! Foreman, I'm ready to go up now. I'm sorry, Foreman. I've been trying to get to the gold down here, but I just can't. For some reason, I just couldn't get into it! I tried and tried, but I —"

"I know."

"You know? How could you know? There was no one else here. But Foreman! I remembered what I was taught! I remembered the Four P's! My trainer taught me well! As soon as it started, I reminded myself about the Purpose, Plan...the...Power... and um. Right! The Pickaxe!"

"I did not teach you that."

"Oh! I know! My old trainer taught me. And I listened, Foreman! I listened! And I reminded myself and I—"

"Ephraim, I know what you've been doing."

"It's 'Preacher.'" *He always forgets my name.*

"But whatever. How could you know? You just got here? And, there's been no one else down here. I would know. They would have come out and helped me when I—" Preacher was talking so quickly, he barely stopped to breathe.

Foreman interrupted him.

"Ephraim. Your name is Ephraim."

"Oh, ho, ho!" Preacher rolled his eyes and smiled.

"I think I'd know my own name!" Preacher pointed his finger at Foreman, shaking and wagging it playfully.

"Thank you, Sir, but I know who I am. I'm Preacher! That's who I am. And I come here to mine the gold and the stones. I know! I've been doing this for years. Then, I bring them up top, shine up some pieces, and tell everyone at the meeting what I found down here. Except...well; except this week. I'm sorry, Sir, but this week, I failed. I don't know what I'm going to do about the meeting. I know, it's in five days. But, the thing is, I...well, I won't have any gold for this week. Sir, I'm sorry. I just could not get more gold out of this mountain!"

It's not like he actually knows my name, so maybe it won't even make a difference that my presentation will get skipped!

"I slugged at it with my axe. I knocked it. I came at this wall with all my might, but I couldn't get any more gold from the mountain. See, Sir. I just won't be able to —."

"Your name is Ephraim and I know you didn't find gold. I was with you."

"With me! There was no one here with me! I was all alo—"

"Alone? You were never alone."

That voice again. There it was. I know that voice.

"You will never, ever be completely alone. I am with you."

"How'd you do that?! I remember that sound from when you were at the top of the mine shaft! It sounded like you were standing right next to me!" A sly smile filled Preacher's face as he turned a squinted eye to Foreman.

"Did you get some type of special sound system installed in the mines?"

"I was here with you."

"There you go again! No one was with me when you first came down the elevator! There was all this light everywhere, but you were up there and I was down here. I know it!"

"How do you know it?"

"I know it because I felt so alone! I was screaming and crying out and obliterating the rock wall. Trust me, no one was anywhere nearby."

"I was with you then, Ephraim."

"It's Preacher, and why do you say that? How could you have been with me?"

"I handed you every axe."

"What do you mean, 'every axe?'"

Foreman's losing his mind, Preacher thought.

"It was just me and my trusty..." Preacher trailed off as Foreman directed his gaze.

All around Preacher, there were more tools than he could count. Axes, chisels, mallets, and hammers were everywhere. They littered the ground, lying haphazardly around Preacher in the cavern of the Gold Gateway.

Preacher gasped.

"Every axe you destroyed, I replaced. You'd strike the rock and destroy the point. Then, you'd set the axe aside. Then, you'd reach over your shoulder for another one, and I'd hand it to you."

"There must be fifty axes here!"

"Axes, chisels, mallets...yes. There are many. You tried every tool you could think of."

"But, how could you have been here without me seeing you?"

"Ephraim, you chose not to see."

"How could I choose not to see you? You're the boss!"

"You chose not to see me because you were looking for the gold. Every decision to chase is a decision to abandon. For the last three days, you've chased gold and abandoned me."

"Three days? It couldn't have been three days! That would mean the meeting is in two!"

"Yes, Ephraim. You have been here for three days...but you have been chasing and abandoning for far longer than that."

"But the meeting?! You've got to help me! There's gold here, I know it! What am I doing wrong?! I see you now! I want your help now! Where should I hit?"

And what did that mean? I've been 'chasing and abandoning' for a long time?
Preacher pushed that thought away.

He picked up one of the axes that was close to him. He ran to the wall where he'd stopped and started to swing. "Is it here?" Preacher pointed to the wall at the same place he would have hit had he kept going. He looked at Foreman with a wildness in his eyes. "Or, no. That's silly. Why would it be here? I've already been here!"

Preacher kept his axe on his shoulder and ran to another place in the wall. "Maybe it's here?!" He looked desperately at Foreman. "Mr. Foreman! Why won't you help me?!"

Preacher reared back with his current axe, with its broken point. "Just tell me where to swing and I'll get to work!" Preacher shoved the other tools out of his way. He winced as the heavy axe handles, steel axe heads, wooden mallets, and iron chisels knocked against his legs and ankles as he shoved them.

Then, he planted his feet and swung the axe.

"Clunk!" The flat of the broken axe didn't even bruise the mountain.

"Ephraim."

Preacher swung again. "Shhhhunk!" And again. "Shhhunk!" And, again! "Shunk." The metal and stone reverberated, but the stone did not budge.

"Ephraim. The mountain won't yield to you this way."

"Oh, right! Thanks! I've got it now. I forgot!" He turned back to the wall.

Preacher straightened up, put the axe down on the ground with an exaggerated appearance of calm. He put a hand on his chest, closed his eyes, and said "Most worthy mountain! I see you! I know you! I'm coming for you!"

Then, Preacher, put on a smile like a person seeing they're about to be unexpectedly photographed. His cheeks lifted, his eyes squinted, but his face showed no humor or true levity.

He lifted his axe, turned, and swung.

"Clump!"

Preacher dropped his gaze. He breathed deeply. Though his mighty hands had lifted the axe for thousands of swings, it seemed to weigh five hundred pounds at this moment. The axe dropped and Preacher just stared at the ground.

His eyes caught the shine of a chisel with a mallet nearby

and his eyes shifted up to the wall.

"Should I—"

"Ephraim."

"That's it isn't it?! I'm using the wrong tools! Gold must be coaxed out, not knocked out. I get it!"

Preacher ran and grabbed at the chisel and positioned it.

"Here we go!" He lifted the mallet just as Foreman called out. "Ephraim!"

In an instant, the mallet flew and found the back of the chisel. Too fast for Preacher to stop it, the chisel slid off the rock and moved sideways. The mallet kept its momentum and Preacher's hand moved forward on the chisel, into the rock wall. It had borne much of the force of the mallet and got pinched between the mallet, the chisel, and the rock! Trying to stop himself, Preacher released his hold on the mallet; but it was too late and that made it worse.

The mallet slid off the chisel, bounced off the wall, and up onto Preacher's chest!

"Ow! ...Ooof!" Preacher yelped.

The chisel clanged to the stony ground.

Confused by what had happened so quickly, and the pain he felt in his hand and chest, Preacher stood still and began to weep silently.

Rubbing his hands together and moving them up to his chest, Preacher stood in one place. He couldn't even move around freely for fear of tripping on the axes and tools around him.

"Why can't I do this?"

He closed his eyes and wept. Then, he lifted his good hand to cover his face while holding the injured hand to his injured chest.

"I'm a miner. This is what I do. But now the very tools I know and use every day are hurting me."

"No."

"What?" Preacher barely turned so the side of his face angled towards Foreman and he could just see him from the corner of his eye.

"What do you mean, 'No?'"

CHAPTER 6: WHO WOULD YOU BE?

Preacher looked up with a start, as realization dawned on him. His eyes searched Foreman's face for some detail, any detail that would reveal his intentions. His mouth wide open, waiting for confirmation.

"Wait, are you firing me?! I knew it!" Preacher turned his face back and closed his eyes again. He brought his hands to cover his mouth in a reflex as old as he was. Shame had no need of introduction and fear needed no directions to get to Preacher's heart.

"Look at me."

Preacher lifted his eyes enough to see Foreman's feet. His eyelids, like the axe before, seemed to weigh tons; and today, his heart was no fulcrum to lift them.

"If you weren't a miner, who would you be?"

"I don't know." Preacher began.

"I don't know what I would do." He continued to cradle his injured hand. "I like mining. Or...I thought I did." Preacher's eyes scanned the floor. The dust, the rubble, the chunks of rock, the axes, the tools and there, in the corner - many feet away - Preacher saw his hard hat.

I won't need that anymore if I'm getting fired, he thought.

"I could help out at the meetings. I could get the pamphlets together. I could organize the samples for people. Maybe I could even help out the—"

"Ephraim. I asked you…"

"I couldn't even do that?!" Preacher interrupted. "You don't want me any more, do you? You don't even want me in your company if I can't be a miner?! Oh no!" Preacher brought his head low again, cradling it between his hands and his chest.

"Ephraim! You are getting in your own way. Listen to me."

"I'm sorry."

"You are not alone. You are Ephraim. You are my child."

The light swelled! It swirled in great ripples and eddies around them. The colors seemed suddenly brighter and more substantial than before. They coursed through the cavern, pouring in and out of every crevice. Now covering the floor like a vibrant lava, splashing and refreshing everything it touched. Now crashing against the walls and spraying up as a liquid pool of radiance.

"It...it was you?"

"Of course it was."

"But..."

"Ephraim. You are my son. I am your Father."

"I...but I..." Preacher stammered. "I couldn't get the gold." His weak hands used the small reserves of energy left in them to motion a mostly bent hand at the walls while looking at Foreman.

"You were never alone, Ephraim. I have been with you."

"But..."

"Ephraim. Who would you be if you were not a miner?"

"I..." Preacher looked at nothing in particular. He stared, mouth open as the colors swirled around the two of them. Then, his eyes caught one thread of blue as it moved in front of him, flying as a spear of light through the sea of metallic yellows and oranges around them. The blue twinkled into a green, then a yellow, into a violet, then back into a crystalline blue as it swirled up and over Foreman. Then, it went into Foreman!

Preacher inhaled sharply.

As quickly as it had entered him, the light came back out of Foreman, more vibrant and with greater fullness! This was no normal light!

This was no normal man! Preacher's eyes rested on Foreman and he blinked away the confusion, like Old Man Winter, shaking off his slumber for the new life of Spring. He focused on

Foreman and noticed his gaze was both intense and kind. Ephraim noticed his smile.

"Y...You..." Ephraim stammered.

Ephraim breathed deep and loud. His shaken breath matched his shaken confidence about the world around him.

"Father?" Through great tears, Ephraim turned his body, lifted his weak arms, and took a step. Suddenly, he was surrounded. The light swelled in intensity and Ephraim was carried forward, even as Father embraced him.

Ephraim was enveloped with light and color, sound and warmth. The classic melody of joy that he'd known from childhood filled Ephraim's heart and mind. Blackberries, pond jumping and swimming, driving his first car, the love of his family filled him. "M...my family!"

"Yes, your family," Father said to him, kindly. "I have been with them, but you will have work to do when you go home. They have missed you and they were concerned until I comforted them."

Ephraim let his mind swim in the embrace of his Father. He pictured each member of his family. Then, thought of his drive to work at the mountain. Then, he remembered...

The mountain!

As Ephraim stood, enfolded in the arms and heart embrace of Father, he remembered his drive to work. He thought of his neighbors with the dog, the grocery store with the new sign, and the farms with their rows and rows of crops. He remembered the last stop on his way out of town and how he used to always pause at that one stop sign at the four corners.

"When did I stop?" Ephraim asked; whether aloud or only in his mind, it didn't matter. Ephraim knew his Father heard him.

"That's unimportant," Father said. "What's important is that you are here with me now."

Ephraim shook with new emotion. "I'm sorry." He clung to Father in desperation, as if he were surrounded by a raging ocean, and Father, the only buoy. "I'm sorry, I'm sorry, I'm sorry."

With pain, remorse, and a thin shining thread of hope, Ephraim remembered and pictured it very clearly. His face beamed as he pulled to the four-way stop in the middle of the fields. He'd turn off the car, get out and walk around to the front. Then, he'd raise his hands and say, "Thank you, Father! I know you are here! You're always with me! I love you! I love that you will never leave me! Please come talk with me today, I'm going to your mountain. Be with my family as I leave them to their day." In the utter solitude of the quiet fields, Ephraim knew he was not alone. As the breezes blew through the crops, he reveled in these moments, confident that there were no other people for miles. Ephraim would talk to Father and even read some of the miner's manual, knowing Father was nearby. And then, smiling, Ephraim would sing the song of the mountain.

"I was so happy." He said as he clung to his Father. "Why?"

"Because you were responding to my invitation." Father said it, holding on to Ephraim just as tightly. "I invited you and you came. Freely and joyfully."

Ephraim tightened his eyes as he pushed his head into Father's chest; an Ephraim gem, embedded in the rock of his Father, never wanting to be removed.

"Do you remember my song? Sing with me."

Where it leads, I'll follow
It's both full and hollow!
Oh, into the mine, I go!

CHAPTER 7: A NEW SONG TO SING

Ephraim thought of the lines he'd rehearsed every day.

"No," Father responded to Ephraim's thoughts. "Begin with me at the start:

"Come, my beloved, join me where I am
I have a purpose; for you, I have a plan

Where I am now, is where you can be
The things that I'm doing, come do them with me!
You've dug with your shovel, and picked with your axe
Now, join me in digging! Take up this light pack!
My mountain is beauty, my mountain brings peace,
Walk with me, talk with me, dig with me, please.
I've answered the Tollbooth, I've paid the great price.
Now you're free to come join me, you're free from the Ice!
I took your place, yes. For you, I chose death.
I picked you for myself. Choose me and draw breath!

Oh, come join my mountain, it's deep and it's tall
Come join my mountain, there's room here for all!
Come walk with me, talk with me, follow my ways,
Come to my mountain, forever, always!"

"Then," Ephraim said, "we answer:

"Oh, King of the mountain, you know what's best
King of the mountain, our answer is 'Yes!'
We join your mountain, we're coming to you!
Whatever you're doing, we will do it with you!
We've dug with our shovels, we were slaves to the Cold,
Now, we'll work with you, King! Your love makes us bold!
We'll walk where you walk, and we'll talk with our King!
We'll work how you tell us, and with you we'll sing...

Ohhhhh, welcome to The Mountain, the hill of the King!
Our burdens are light now, He's changed everything!
Take his hand, and walk with him
It's better here, you'll see!
The King of the Mountain
Loves you and he loves me!"

"Oh, Father!" Ephraim cried. "Thank you! Thank you for coming to rescue me! Thank you!"

"You're welcome, Ephraim."

"I have a question."

"Yes, Ephraim."

"I remember when I first arrived at the mountain, things were different! I was so happy to be here, and when I'd show up, you would meet me, and we would walk and talk...but something is different. The mountain seems so..." Ephraim paused.

I can't say it. Even using this word near Father seems so wrong. He's going to get mad and leave me down here again! With Father, everything is so full, rich, radiant and beautiful! How can I use this word without upsetting him?

"You do not need to be afraid, Ephraim."

"Well," *Here goes.* "Everything seems so dark now!"

There, now I've said it. Surely he didn't mean I could say that and it would be fine!

There was nothing dark about Father.

"Ephraim, open your eyes."

Ephraim had forgotten he was still in the embrace of Father. He'd even forgotten that his eyes were closed!

How much time has passed?! How long have we stayed like this?

"Do I have to?"

"Please; Ephraim. Open your eyes. I want you to see something with your eyes, not just your heart."

Ephraim found that he had to give conscious thought to opening his eyes. It was as if his body, itself, did not want anything to change either.

I've never had to think about opening my eyes before! Now, it's harder than picking up my axe!

Eventually, Ephraim opened his eyes.

In an instant, Ephraim hugged Father tightly again as he recoiled.

"What is this?! Why is everything so strange?! Where are we?"

"Ephraim, we have not moved."

"But, but…But everything is so bright! I don't understand!"

"Ephraim," Father said with a smile, "do you remember your first day here at my mountain?"

"I do. Yes." Ephraim said.

"Where did we go on your first day?"

"Oh, I loved that! We took the elevator up to the top of the mountain! You showed me the view of the fields, the town, my house, and all the surrounding cities! It was amazing!"

"I'm so glad you liked it!"

"Oh yes! I remember it well, now!" Ephraim said suddenly. "The first day!"

"Yes?" Father invited more.

"Well, we walked around for a while up top…and…and then we came back down and you told me how we would work together that day."

"And where was that? Do you remember, Ephraim?"

"I do! It was on the first floor of the mountain!"

"That's right, Ephraim. I'm glad you remember that."

"You said the things I did with you would change my town. Also, that it would change me. You said it would change me and I would go up from level to level on the mountain - as I worked on it."

"Did I?"

"I guess I must have done really bad work to have ended up here in this deep layer underground." Ephraim looked around, confused. "But everything is sure different now!"

"Ephraim, I didn't say the work you do would change you. What I said was that working with me would change you! That's how ice-life functions. That's how the ice people of your town think. They strive to change by *doing*. In my mountain, you change - not by the work you do, but by your nearness to me."

"I...I don't understand."

"Ephraim, it's not the work that changes you. When you and all the other miners go up from level to level, it's not from the sweat of your brow or the throw of the axe."

"It's not?"

"It's from your connection to me. When you all, with your faces freed from the ice - talk with me, think of me, stay near to me. Then, I move you from level to level."

"Oh no!" Ephraim brought his hand to his face immediately. He felt around on his cheeks and chin. "Wait! Was the ice growing on me again? Is that why you put me down there so low in the tunnel? Because I've gone back to being held by the ice?"

"Ephraim, you will never be captive to the ice again." He said it so firmly, that it almost made Ephraim afraid.

"Ever. I died. I took the worst the Ice king could deal out. And I am here again. If I free you - or anyone - from the ice, they are free."

Ephraim was relieved. He sighed and kept listening.

"Still, Ephraim, even though you did not become captive to the ice again, you started to behave like you had. Ephraim, you stopped talking with me. You stopped walking with me. You stopped singing with me and the other miners."

"Ephraim, your face was beginning to grow cold. It's not that you would have become captive to the ice like you once were, but you...well, Ephraim - look at where we are."

"I don't understand where we are." Ephraim scanned the room all around him. He looked up and squinted. "It's so bright! I mean, it was bright before, but now it's brighter still! And Father, why are those axes up there?" Ephraim pointed to axes, strewn all over the ceiling. There were axes and chisels, mallets, and rocks that were on the ceiling.

"I almost feel like...are we..." Just then, Ephraim's eyes caught his hard hat over in a corner. "It's on the ceiling...on the ceiling!"

"Are we upside down?" Ephraim clung to Father and looked in horror at the floor beneath his feet. "I don't understand!"

"Ephraim, it is only now that we are right-side-up!"

CHAPTER 8: SAVING FACE
AND LOSING FATHER'S

    With the new understanding of where he was, Ephraim looked around the room differently. He started to notice things he hadn't noticed before. Rock piles were on the ceiling now. His hat, his axes, his other tools...all on the ceiling.

"But, why is it so bright, now? The mountain is upside down and the lights are on? This doesn't seem right."

"Ephraim," Father said it with a weight that had not characterized his voice before; not in the same way. "Ephraim, nothing has changed in the mountain. What has changed here, is you."

"I did this?!" Ephraim asked.

"In a sense, you are responsible for this change; yes," said Father.

"Wow!" Ephraim looked around in awe. The lights dimmed a little, right as Father said, "Ephraim!"

He snapped back to facing Father. Ephraim's eyes betrayed the fear he felt; the awe with which he looked at Father.

The light in the tunnel grew brighter.

"Ephraim. What did you feel in your heart just then?"

"Power." Ephraim said it flatly.

"And this is the problem." Father went on. "Ephraim, when I told you that you were partly responsible for the change in the tunnel, you felt power. More than feeling power, though, you believed the power was yours to command."

"Ephraim, my son. The responsibility you have is that you darkened the tunnel. That is, Ephraim, you believed the tunnel to be dark. So, for you, it was dark. Your mind was darkened by your thoughts, so your world became darker to match them. Ephraim, you were responsible for the tunnel being so dark, so cold, so hopeless, so confusing, so scary."

Ephraim's eyes grew wide.

"It was your mind, darkened as it was, that made the tunnel so bleak...and every day, you went into the tunnel believing you needed a headlamp. All this because you were responsible for it."

"But...but how?!" Ephraim asked.

"You, turned away from me, Ephraim." Father put his hand on Ephraim's shoulder. "The first day you came to the tunnel and didn't bother asking me to join you; it was then that you turned away from me."

"Wait! I remember that day!" Ephraim cut in. "I remember I just wanted to get to work so I could be done. I didn't understand why the tunnel seemed dark that day." Ephraim looked up. "I was so confused! When I got into the elevator, it went down and I didn't even bother to ask why! I just wanted to get the work done. So, I got out, and started digging. It was dark, so I went back up the elevator and grabbed a hard hat with a lamp!"

"Yes, Ephraim. That is what happened." Father's eyes quivered. He was grieved.

"On that day, you came to the mountain to work. You didn't come to meet me. You didn't come to walk with me or talk with me. You didn't come to sing my song. You went...to get gems. So, your tunnel was darker. Your work was harder. You needed a lamp because you weren't looking for me. When I am with you, you don't need a light, or a lamp, or even the sun! But without me, you don't realize the darkness you invite."

"But I thought you said you'd never leave me!" Ephraim was not accusatory, but confused.

"Good for you, Ephraim. You are right." Ephraim smiled with appreciation of the affirmation. Still, his confusion remained. "I told you I'd never leave you and I didn't. I was right here with you all the time."

"So, why was it dark? And why was it upside down?"

"Yes. Ephraim, your mind was dark, the world around you was not. Your vision was darkened, the tunnel was not - because I was with you."

"But how did I get upside down?"

"Ephraim, you turned yourself that way."

Ephraim merely blinked in his confusion.

"Ephraim, that day, you went into the tunnel and you

thought it was without me. I was with you, but you didn't see me, you saw only the rocks, tools, and gems. You did not look for me, and you did not acknowledge me or talk with me through it. So, what was once a delight for us together became work for you. That is the way of all struggles that exclude me and don't include a relationship with me."

"So, I turned upside down?"

"You did. If you were to see it now, you might find it funny, but I assure you, it was no laughing matter at the time. You kept your head down and started to contort yourself to go on the elevator. I didn't want you to get hurt, so I allowed you to float…"

"Upside down?!" Ephraim's hand was on his forehead again. He kept his eyes locked on Father, around his arm that didn't leave his head. Ephraim was incredulous. "And I've been upside down ever since?"

"Most of the time you spent in the mountain, yes."

"But, why did you let me stay like that?!"

"Ephraim, I told you I would never leave you. I never will."

"But I was making things miserable for myself and I had to be making it hard for others, too!"

"You were. Yes. But Ephraim, I…"

"Wait, I'm so sorry. Please forgive me." Ephraim's face flushed as he realized he'd just interrupted Father.

"Sorry. I just…"

"Go on."

"I was darkened in my thoughts because I stopped looking for you. So, I needed a lamp for my work in the mountain…Is that right?"

"Yes. That's right."

"And then, because I was confused, I started to turn myself upside down?" Ephraim was astonished.

"And while I was upside down, you used your power to provide for me and protect me?"

"Yes, Ephraim."

"So I wouldn't hurt myself?"

"Or others," Father said, "yes."

Ephraim just stared, unmoving, at Father. "But I really thought the whole mountain where I worked was underground! From that day 'til this moment, I thought I worked underground! I told everyone I worked underground! I thought it was a dark - dark as the darkest night - tunnel that went farther and farther underground!"

"For you, it did."

"What?"

"Ephraim, I kept you supported as you worked in the self-imposed darkness. But, Ephraim, I also kept you upside down by making the whole mountain function for you while you were upside down. You never knew the difference!"

"You provided for me while I was hurting you?"

Father acknowledged it, "Yes Ephraim. I did. That's what never leaving means. It's what it means to never forsake you. Not just that I watch when you hurt yourself apart from me, but that I provide for you and move mountains when you need it."

"I didn't even know you could do all that!"

"Could?"

"I didn't know you had that much power!"

The lights dimmed again.

"Wait! I'm staring at you!"

"It was only the light in you that dimmed, Ephraim. You didn't take your eyes off me, but you failed to believe the right things about me. The same things result. Wait until you see me as I really am!"

"I look forward to that day," Ephraim agreed.

Then Ephraim shook his head. "I just don't understand it."

"What don't you understand?"

"How is it good for you to care for me when I was dishonoring you?"

"What do you mean, 'good for me,' Ephraim?"

"Well, I always heard that the King of the Mountain did what was best for his own name and shine." Ephraim was hesitant to continue.

"Go on."

"Well, it's just...how is it good for you if you care for me when I'm forgetting you?!"

"Ephraim, I am not like other people you know."
"Well, that's for sure!"

Father smiled.

He went on, "Ephraim, I don't need to keep people impressed with me. I'm seeking hearts, not fans. Hearts that love, not fans who like me while I make them happy."

"Oh? Okay."

"And Ephraim,"

"Yes?"

"Ephraim, you don't have to either."

"I don't have to what?"

"You don't have to save face, Ephraim. You can be who you are."

"But people will…"

"Ephraim, it was saving face that got you upside down and in the dark."

"But how?"

"Ephraim, on that day, do you remember why you were in a hurry to be done?"

"No. Why?"

"Ephraim, you were comparing yourself to another miner."

Ephraim's face was flat. He showed no emotion and no sign that he could remember what Father had told him.

Ephraim said nothing.

"Oh no! The miner's meetings!"

"Yes, Ephraim."

"I had been listening to the recordings of all the other miners and their presentations. Then, I came across one who had done a great job! He had dug up gold!"

"Yes?"

"Yes! Gold!"

"And?"

"And, people were flocking to his presentations! Hundreds! Thousands! I wanted…to be like him." Ephraim started to look down.

"Ephraim! I am here and I love you. You will never be alone."

Ephraim looked up. He continued.

"Yes! Yes, that's right. I wanted to be like the other miner after hearing his presentation and seeing the crowds. So, then, I wanted to find gold too."

"But that's not all."

"It's not?

"No. You didn't just want to be like him. Did you?"

"No...I didn't."
"What did you want?"

"I felt badly that he'd found gold. I wanted to find some, too."

"Why?"

"I had only found some boring copper the day before and nothing special for many days before."

"Ephraim, what difference does it make?"

"People know! People care! Miners know!"

"Well, Ephraim, I know some do. But really, for you to compare yourself with others out of fear of what they're thinking of you...it's a trap. Do you see that?"

"Kind of?"

"Do you?"

"Well, I don't like how it feels, but...I guess, no. Please tell me."

"That is a very good response." Father smiled at Ephraim.

Then, Father said "Ephraim, the only miners who would care about your dig results or the shine of the gems are the miners who, like you, have lost track of where I am. They are miners who have stopped looking to me. Worst of all, they have stopped walking with me, talking with me, and Ephraim, listen to this... those are the ones who are also upside down in their focus and upside down in their tunnels."

Ephraim opened his mouth as wide as he could make it and his eyes were bulging towards Father.

"There are others?"

"Yes, Ephraim. There are others who, this very moment, are upside down. They believe that they work in a dark cavern."

"Others who you preserve while they are upside down?!"

"Yes, Ephraim, there are many miners who are upside-down in their caves throughout the world."

"That's amazing!"

"Amazing?"

"Yes! I mean, I'm sorry for them, but it's amazing what you can do for so many of us at the same time!"

"Ephraim, please understand. There is nothing I cannot do. There is nothing that does not ultimately belong to me. Yes, I preserved you upside-down for many days. But, Ephraim, there's so much more.

> Mine is the axe you use to carve. Mine was
> the lamp to light your way.
> Mine is the rock you axe and chop. Mine's the
> night of the cave and the light of the day.
> Mine is the mountain, whose depths you
> plumb. Mine, the air you breathe.
> Mine is the wall you labor on. Mine are the

people you aim to please.
Mine are the maps you followed here. Mine,
the secrets of this place.
Mine are the successes you hold so dear. Mine, the
light which now brightens your face."

"Ephraim," Father smiled again. "I have no peers."

"There is no one I need to impress. No one whose opinions I must shape. Ephraim, I did not lose face by sustaining you while you forgot me."

"But what about all the people we are recruiting? Don't you want them to think well of you? Don't you want to show them your power?"

"Ephraim, I'm picky about displays of power. Very seldom does power change a heart.

Power wows and woos, but it doesn't win.
Backs bow and bend under pressure; they don't yield or give in.
The people I want are invited and loved.
They're forgiven and beckoned to join me above.
See, my mountain is not filled by displays of force,
I invite friends to be with me without regret or remorse."

Father continued, "When you were trying to save face, you lost sight of mine. But for me, when I set aside my own reputation, I gained by loving you so much and keeping my word to be with you always."

Father beamed and the rock rippled as a wave shook the mountain.

"What was that?!" Ephraim cried as he scanned the ceiling and the walls around him.

"This is the hill of my joy." Father smiled. "The rocks rejoice with me when I rejoice in them!"

"I always thought those quakes were dangerous! I thought they were signs that the rock was unstable!"

"Unstable?" Father smiled. "The rocks delight in the delight I have. They couldn't be more stable, Ephraim.

> They sway with my rhythm. They dance in my song.
> They hum when I grin. They shine all night long!
> The rocks and the earth, and the trees and the wind;
> Ephraim, I made them!
> And they ring with my hymns."

A tear formed in Ephraim's eye. "There's so much I don't know."

"Yes! I know! Isn't it wonderful?!" Father's smile grew even wider! "You are so ignorant of so many things!"

Ephraim looked at Father. His half-smile fixed in place as he slightly turned his head.

"It's good that I'm..." He couldn't bring himself to say it. "I'm...that I...don't know things?"

"Ignorant!" Father called with a smile. "I said, 'ig...nor... ant!'" He howled with laughter!

Ephraim could only stare up at Father with a confused, open-mouthed grin. It was hard to be hurt when Father was obviously so happy.

"Ephraim. Are you afraid?"

"No." Ephraim shook his head while his smile lingered.

"Ephraim," Father tilted his head forward while still smiling. "Are you afraid of being foolish?"

"I..." Ephraim balked. His eyes fell away from Father. "I... I..."

"Ephraim. Are you afraid of being foolish?"

"I'm afraid of being a fool." Ephraim shut his eyes and covered his brow with his hand.

"That is a very brave answer," Father said. Through his closed eyes and covered face, Ephraim could tell that the light in the mountain grew brighter around him.

"Ephraim," Father began, "I am your Father. Ephraim... with me, you don't have to be afraid of not knowing anything." Ephraim breathed in a deep breath.

"Ephraim, I know you don't know everything. I expect you to not know things. Your ignorance, with humility to know it, and then an invitation to be taught by me...that is the most delightful red carpet you could roll out for me to come to your side."

Ephraim continued to stand still with his eyes closed, breathing slowly.

"But it's not me you're afraid of, is it, Ephraim?" Ephraim's face turned into a scowl with his eyes closed tighter.

Slowly, Ephraim shook his head to the sides.

"Yes." Father said. "Worship lingers long in the hearts of men."

Ephraim opened his eyes and looked at Father. "Worship?"

"Worship, Ephraim."

"But I didn't worship my father. I didn't worship the Ice King. I didn't worship my boss or my coworkers. I don't worship my wife." Ephraim's tears glistened with the waves of colors flowing around them.

"Worship is what the heart does when it yields itself. Worship is what the mind does when it gives over its own will to the will of another."

Ephraim's mind swam. He pictured all the people he'd ever looked up to. Comic book heroes came into his mind. Jimmy and Mike, neighbors from down the street; growing up. Ephraim remembered his little orange hot rod that never left his pocket as a child. Even his favorite coin, on his bookshelf, when he was seven. Countless celebrities, the mayor, his first crush, even his children came into Ephraim's mind. Then, he imagined many of them fading back into a dark fog while some faces and pictures stayed bright and clear in Ephraim's mind.

He snapped his eyes open. "How can I get rid of them? They're all over my mind...and my heart."

Father smiled. "That is a very good question, Ephraim. I'm glad you asked."

"You cannot change the past."

"What?!" Ephraim held his hands up, he shrugged in a yielding pose. "So, it's hopeless?" He held back tears.

"Oh, no." Father smiled. "Hope is how I brought you here. Hope is the polish for the gems, Ephraim.

> You cannot change the past; it's true.
> But you can change the way it changes you!"

"I don't understand."

"Fantastic! I knew you wouldn't!" Father grinned.

"Follow me." Father turned to walk away.

"But I..." Ephraim stammered.

"This way." Father looked over his shoulder and beckoned Ephraim, who shuffled and started walking. "Let's take those off." Father pointed at Ephraim's feet and his boots fell away.

"But the rock!" Ephraim argued.

Smiling, Father said, "Ha! Ephraim, have you ever walked on this ceiling before?"

"No."

"Well, there's a lot less gravel here; and no tools. And now," He pointed to the ceiling and smiled again, "you're right side up." Father started walking. He hummed as he stepped.

"But what does walking have to do with my...my past?"

"Oh look! Look at that, your hard hat!" Father pointed at it.

Ephraim looked at it as he walked. He remembered the lamp and how big of a deal it had seemed when it first broke.

"What do you think of that?!" Father asked about the hat; he nodded at it to punctuate the question.

"It's my hat."

"Yup! Your hat! Do you want me to fix the lamp for you?"

"It's on the ceiling."

"I can reach it! Do you want me to fix it?"

"No, that would be silly now. I'm right-side up, and I don't need the lamp any more."

"Hmm!" Father said, smiling as he walked on. Ephraim looked at Father and squinted. "Let's pick up the pace!" Father started to jog. He turned to Ephraim as he jogged forward.

"Careful! You'll run into that wall!" Ephraim pointed.

"Hmm?" Father feigned confusion about Ephraim's words as he kept moving, faster even!

"Stop!"

CHAPTER 9: THIS WEEK'S WORK AND THIS WEEK'S TREASURE

Father disappeared into the side of the mountain as Ephraim pulled up short to a stop. He scanned the rock face and pressed various places all over the rock in confusion.

A hand reached from the rock and pulled him forward. Ephraim yelped: "Aahhh!"

Suddenly, Ephraim found himself standing in the rock.

"Where are we?" Ephraim whispered, looking around, confused. *I'm standing in the mountain! Inside the mountain! In the rock!*

"We're in the mountain, like we've always been!" Father smiled at him.

"But that's not possible!"

"Oh? I thought it was." Father smiled. He leaned over to Ephraim and whispered, "Should we leave?"

Ephraim stared around in wonder. He couldn't believe what he was seeing! The colors swirled everywhere, just as they had since Father called from above...or below. Behind the colors, Ephraim knew he was standing inside of rock. He moved his hands in front of him.

"It's not water," Father said. "It's rock."

Ephraim looked at Father. No change had come over the rock. Ephraim could tell it was still just as much rock as it had been. What had changed, though, was Ephraim could stand inside it. As he stared, he noticed the rock was everywhere he expected it to be, but he could see through it. When he turned to the path they'd come from, Ephraim could see the grey, shadowy rock gave way to a lighter color that made up the path.

He turned to Father who was smiling as he looked at Ephraim. He'd been patiently waiting as Ephraim looked around.

"This...This is amazing!" Ephraim said it looking at Father and holding his arms out wide.

As he turned, the tips of Ephraim's fingers touched the

boundary of rock and air and he pulled them in sharply. "Ooh! It's cold!" Ephraim rubbed his finger tips. That's when it dawned on him. "Wait! My hand doesn't hurt any more!" He looked at Father through the rock. "And, the rock is warm!"

"How is it that the rock is warmer than the air in the mountain? I always thought it was the rock that was colder than the air!"

"There are many things you once thought that will change with me, Ephraim." Father smiled. "And yes, the rock wanted to heal your hand after you hit it on the chisel. So, I let it."

"The rock healed me?"

"I healed you. The rock asked for it. I granted it."

"You talk to the rock?"

"Does that surprise you? I know the language of everything I have made."

"You talk to the rock?!"

Father smiled. "Not like we're talking, no. But yes. I commune with the rock." Ephraim's eyes were wide in awe. He said, "This is your mountain! The hill of your joy!"

"You've got it." Father held his arms wide open and smiled. "Now," Father beamed, "let's keep going!" Father waved Ephraim on and started jogging.

As Ephraim jogged and caught up to stay near Father, he was amazed at everything he saw! The swirling colors kept pace with Father, like waves circling a massive galleon on the sea. Everywhere Father went, the light followed, dancing around him, sometimes splashing up against him in a twinkling spray of light. Sometimes, it seemed to course through Father! One thing he noticed clearly, the light always flowed out from Father, originating from him. Still, Ephraim noticed that while it seemed Father was the source, and the light flowed away from him, the radiant river flowed out, through the rock, and then came back to Father. It always came back to Father, like Father was its source and its destination; its commander and its port.

Ephraim smiled as he watched. Never before had light so captivated him. As he watched the light, Ephraim also noticed that the rock was not uniform. *Of course!* He thought. *The rock is as diverse as it's always been! There's shale and soil, individual pebbles and stones. There are tiny gems and massive boulders!*

Each rock had its own unique translucence. As he got closer to passing through a rock, Ephraim noticed that the borders became clear and what he thought was a uniform grey mass was actually a thousand separate rocks and soils.

I'm running through rock with my Father.

"Going up!" Father called out. Suddenly, Ephraim noticed he was angling up, running to another level! The layers began to change as they ran through them. The density and translucence of the layers were unique to this level, as well!

"What is this?!" Ephraim called to Father. "Is this what you always do?" *I'm not out of breath! I'm running uphill, through rock and shale, gems and soil; and I'm not out of breath!*

"Sometimes!" Father said. "I do enjoy a good run through my mountain!"

They ran up through the layer above them. The layer Ephraim once thought was below. Ephraim's eyes swam as he took in the beauty of the rocks through which he ran. Seeing them from inside was a unique delight he'd never even imagined.

Then, as they ran, Father said "Ephraim, what are you worshiping right now?"

"I...I'm not worshiping anything right now."

"Really? You're running under the ceiling you once called the floor. You're breathing well while passing through rock. You're following me with light you never knew existed. You're doing the impossible, Ephraim; and it's all because I invited you and you joined me."

"Ok!" Ephraim called. They were running fast now. Faster than Ephraim had ever run in his life. "But what does that have to do with worship?!"

"Haha! Everything!" Father ran faster. Ephraim caught up. Faster! Ephraim caught up.

Then, turning with a smile to Ephraim, Father zoomed ahead! He ran so fast that Ephraim couldn't catch him. Trails of light followed Father and the whole mountain seemed to ignite in a ring of cool and beautiful fire as it encircled the whole level.

Ephraim slowed to a stop.

"Are...you...afraid?" Father's voice came from the trails of light.

"No, Father." Ephraim watched as the light pulsated. It grew bright and dulled, grew bright and dulled in the arc nearby that faded in the distance as it bent around inside the mountain. By the slight arc and angle, Ephraim assumed the mountain was very large. Ephraim could tell when Father ran past him because the light brightened with his approach, peaked, and dimmed the slightest bit, as he passed.

Suddenly, the light trails faded completely. Ephraim stood alone in the rock with only the original rivers of light that had erupted when he recognized Father's arrival.

"Are you afraid, now, Ephraim?" Father's voice seemed to be hundreds of paces away.

Ephraim smiled. "No, Father. I'm not afraid now. I know you're here."

Then, the light went out. The rivers of amber, red, topaz, sapphire, violet; the twinkling green flourish in the waves of cool fire - all blinked out.

"And now?" The voice seemed even farther away; barely audible.

Ephraim's smile dropped with the light. He stood in a familiar cave darkness. Memories of the last time he was in the dark flooded Ephraim's thoughts.

The axe, the lamp, the hard hat, the wall. The futility. The pounding on the walls to get the gold. The elevator. Ephraim could see himself in his mind's eye, pitifully crouching in the dark, holding his hand, in fear and despair because his plans had failed and the elevator had left.

Ephraim remembered the elevator and the corner of his mouth lifted with the sense of hope that rose in his mind. *The elevator!*
Father came up the elevator. Up. Up and not down. Father brought light and a song for me. When I was lost in the mine shaft, Father brought hope and helped me see the way things are supposed to be. He helped me see the way things are.

"Hello Father." Ephraim spoke it aloud.

None but the closest ear could have heard his voice. The calm and quiet with which Ephraim breathed out the words were so peaceful.

"Hello, Ephraim." Father's voice was calm. Father was here.

"You knew I was here."

"Yes, Father. I remembered."

"Ephraim, to follow me, because of me, is to worship me." He went on. "To know that I am with you, because I said I would never leave you; that is to worship me. Ephraim, to trust me when you cannot see and hold onto me when you can barely remember my voice or see evidence of my presence. That is to worship me."

"You will never see the dark the same way again, Ephraim. It may scare you for a moment, but you have bathed in my light. Shadows you see will concern you more because you have seen true light, but you will never have to fear the way you once did."

"So, I think I understand." Ephraim said.

"Yes." Father said. It was not a question or an invitation, but a statement.

"I think I understand now about worship."

"Yes, I think you do."

"I can never change who I was or what I did in the past. The past is done and I can't reach back there. What I can do, though, is worship you. Follow you, hold onto you, even when it's hard...and then, I'll see the past differently."

"Yes." Father said. "Are you angry at yourself for your mistakes in the dark?"

"No. Not angry, Father." He paused. "I believed you were good - even then...but now I have seen and experienced you differently. My fear took over and my pain blinded me...but I'm not angry. That wouldn't help anything. Now, I'm just glad that you've shown me what is true. I'm full of joy and hope because I have a new past that has changed who I am. The new past has changed how the old one shaped me."

"Very good." Father smiled. "Like layers of rock you have now seen through, your past is layered. You, however, are not stuck in time. You continue to make a new past with every moment you exist. The question is not what to do with your past, but what you will do with the past you are now creating. How you see the old is shaped by how you have built on it since. Who you become is based on how you choose now. Choose me, Ephraim.

Stay with me."

Suddenly, the light came back with a melody. An instrument like an oboe could be heard, playing in perfect tune with the colors Ephraim saw. They thrilled him.

As he smiled and listened, Ephraim's chest swelled as he breathed. His eyes took in the colors and the ripples. Then, he realized that not one, but two songs were being played by two instruments. *No...three. There are three instruments! Something like an oboe, but more pure and rich. Something like a French horn, but with an audible fullness!* Then, there was something like a cello, with lower lows and velvet notes, that poured into the rock as the colors flew by him.

"Now music, too?"

"There has always been music. You did not always listen."

"Is there more than light, sound, and music?"

"Oh, much, much more." Father closed his eyes and listened as he smiled.

The two stood and drank in the beauty without speaking. Father was the source and the One who most enjoyed it. Ephraim was the observer and happy participant in the orchestral feast that ignited the stone and all he could see around him.

After some time had passed, Father spoke, "Should we stay here?"

Ephraim looked at Father. His face was still smiling and his eyes were still closed, enjoying the music.

"Can you still see the light with your eyes closed?" Ephraim asked.

Father responded,
"I see light you cannot imagine.
I hear music that's never been played.
And yes, Ephraim, my son whom I love.

I enjoy everything my hands have made."

Ephraim looked in wonder. *How could I have ever mistaken Father as just a foreman of the mountain?*

"Please." Ephraim asked with tears beginning to form. "Please help me to never forget and never leave you."

"That," Father said proudly. "That is the best request you have made, so far."

As Ephraim received Father's words, he noticed a light in the distance that shimmered in a special way.

"Father. What is that?"

"Let's go see!"

Ephraim could not comprehend all this day had entailed. His heart was so full, he didn't know it was possible to feel the way he did. His mind swam with new thoughts about the Father, his work, the last few years of his work in the mines...that turned out to be the fullness of the mountain. Again, Ephraim thought of how he was running through rock without any problem and with no boots or hat to protect him! Everything about how he saw things had changed! Still, he ran.

Ephraim could hear what sounded like laughter as Father ran ahead of him. Father was always faster and happier than Ephraim, and he was just fine with that.

When Father slowed down, the trails of light behind him thickened and Ephraim could tell something was changing. He felt the change before his eyes beheld it. "Ooh, it's cold here."

"Is it?" Father asked?

As he prepared to answer, Ephraim realized that, no. The temperature was just right. "Ah...no. No, Father, it's perfect the way it is."

"Wonderful!"

"I'm seeing things differently, Father."

"Yes! Yes you are!" Father laughed. There was no scorn, but a playful recognition of irony.

"These rocks remind me of the light surrounding you!" Ephraim looked at Father with wonder.

All day I have been spending this time with my Father. He has sung to me, sung with me, shown me light. He has healed me and shown me His power. Father has made me see things differently and walked me through walls! We've run and I've seen trails of the light of my Father as he ran! I understand my Father better! I understand myself better! I have seen my past differently! I have a new perspective on my fellow miners! This day is amazing! I am so very thankful!

"Thank you, Father. I'm so grateful for You in my life."

"And I am so happy you're here with me, Ephraim." Father pulled him in for an embrace. Then, he pulled away and pointed Ephraim to the wall. "Have one."

"One of those? They're awfully big. What are they?"

"I'll help you"

"Oh, they're stuck in there pretty well!" Ephraim tugged on the rock in front of him. "Its odd shape really makes it show your light well. It's too bad it's so foggy and dull."

"Oh, you can't take it that way, Ephraim." Father said. His face looked curious at Ephraim's manner of attempting to pull it out by hand. "Sing to it, Ephraim."

"Ok! What should I say?"

"What is in your heart right now?"

"Gratitude. But I don't know any songs of gratitude."

"Just try. I'm with you. I'll never leave you alone, Ephraim. I love you."

Ephraim's heart strengthened inside him. He had never flexed his heart before, but now Ephraim felt as though he could tighten and loosen the strength of his heart and the courage of his chest like any other muscle he controlled. It was new and so satisfying.

"When you say that, Father...everything in me responds." Ephraim had one hand on his chest, looking at Father and feeling his courage bursting forth.

Father responded,

> "Yes. I can strengthen the weakest knees. I
> can embolden the timid heart.
> I can sing and give wings to these, your
> feeble, failing, broken parts.
> I made you and I can build you anew! I can speak life to your soul.
> When you are with me, you find life each day!
> I take broken pieces and, again, make you whole.
> Sing, Ephraim."

Ephraim sang,
> "I...am thankful!"

He looked at Father. Ephraim had always repeated the songs he heard and the lyrics of others. Even with Father, his songs were responses to the truthful words he heard from Father first.
Father smiled at him and nodded and Ephraim continued.

> "I am thankful for this day. My Father rescued me.
> I am here and want to say..."

Ephraim looked in panic at Father. Father was still smiling. His smile spoke the same joy as he'd had all day. This revealed his complete confidence in Ephraim, who continued.

"I once thought I was free!
But now I see Father's face again,
There's beauty I'd not known!
My Father, how he loves me so
He's shown, and shown, and shown!

Never will he leave me here.
Never, will he forsake!
Though all the world abandon me
Though all the world should break!

I know that I'm my Father's child
I have no need of fear!
I know, the best thing that I do
Is to love and keep Him near!

I'll talk with Him,
I'll walk with Him.
My Father is my friend.
And if His hand will hold to me,
My joy will never end!"

Ephraim opened his eyes and breathed in a gasp. He looked around for Father.

"I'm here."

Ephraim could hear the smile in his voice, even as Father spoke.

"Father, what happened? Did you move us? Where are you?"

"No, Ephraim. Look again."

Ephraim looked around. He was surrounded by the rocks he had hoped to pull from the wall. The cavern in which they stood was now bare, and there were piles and piles of the rocks all around them.

"Father! You took them out while I sang?!"

"No, Ephraim. They leapt from the walls as you sang. Each of these yearned and begged to be released from the wall as you sang your song."

"No pickaxe!"

"No pickaxe, Ephraim."

"No chisel."

"No chisel, Ephraim. The soil and rock of the wall released each rock and they slid down in piles."

"There must be thousands of these!"

"Tens of thousands, Ephraim."

"What are they, Father? What are these stones?

"Ephraim, these are diamonds."

"Diamonds?" Ephraim turned to look at Father. He had to push a pile of the stones out of his way to see clearly.

Seeing Father's face, Ephraim checked to make sure he had not misheard. "Like, diamonds, diamonds?"

"Is there another kind?" Father asked, as he smiled.

The knowing smile Ephraim had come to recognize in his Father was usually comforting. This time, Ephraim was confused by it.

Now what do I do? These are not the diamonds I'm used to.

Ephraim looked at the massive rock in his hands. He furrowed his brow. *It probably weighs seven to ten pounds. If it were like the diamonds I'm thinking of, it would be worth a fortune. It's really too bad.*

"Ephraim, is something wrong?"

Ephraim snapped his face up. Looking straight at Father, his jaw dropped. He stammered. "I...I don't..."

What can I say? These are big. They're huge! But they're not diamonds. These...are worthless. They're cloudy. They're dim. They twinkle, but like seeing the sun through mud. Everything I've seen so far has been amazing! I've walked through walls; run through them, really! I've turned upside down, well, been made right from being upside down. What can I say? What can I say?

"Thank...you...Father."

"You're welcome, Ephraim." Father smiled.

He knows. Aaagh! He knows something's wrong. What is wrong with me? Can't I just accept a gift?

"Well, Ephraim, I'll tell you what, why don't you take an extra one."

An extra burden? What should I say?
"Ok, I will."

"Ephraim, these will be here just for us to enjoy together. They're now a part of your past." Father smiled. "They're part of your past but we can meet here sometime in the future. For now, though, why don't we head back down."

"Head back down? Okay."

A little disappointed, Ephraim picked up another of what Father called diamonds. Carrying both of them, he followed Father out.

Ephraim looked back at the cave and the piles of diamonds that Father had let him sing out of the rock walls. *How will I get back there in the future?*

"Ephraim," He looked at Father. "I've enjoyed our time together. Have you?"

"Oh, yes! I really did!"

"I'm glad. And Ephraim, let's talk about the all-hands meeting as we walk back."

The all-hands meeting! How could I forget? "Ok! When is it Father?"

"Three days."

Ephraim couldn't believe what he was hearing.

"Three days!" *I thought it was four! But...well, I also thought we were in here for years!*

"Let's talk."

Father's always so calm! "Ok."

"Tell me about the diamond."

The diamond?! He wants to talk about the diamond? "Ok, well, it's heavy."

"Good. Tell me more. Tell me everything you can see and know about this diamond."

This, I can do! Ephraim described the diamonds in his hands. As he began, he fell into a rhythm he was used to. *This is what I do with everything I brought up from the mines...er... everything I brought down. When I was upside down. Aagh! Anyway! I know what I'm doing now.*

Ephraim took out his pocket tools and took measurements. He described the shape of each one, the points, the rounded features, and the lines. He talked about the colors reflected in the stone, the shadow it cast, and the hardness.

"Great! Tell me about where it came from."

Excellent! This is the only time I love history, when it helps me understand the jewels and stones I find!

Ephraim began to describe the cavern where the diamond had been. He described the height of the cavern's ceiling. He described the setting of each diamond and the way each stone was positioned in the wall. Then, Ephraim described the history of the stone. Based on the color of the wall, the porosity and the moisture content, he could deduce certain things about the history of the diamonds. He understood how they were formed, why they were formed, and what was going on around them when they were formed.

"What difference does it make...for the diamond?"

Without looking away from the diamond, Ephraim began to describe the way the diamond protruded from the wall.

"The shine of the diamond depended on the way it sat and the angle it held. The walls…"

Ephraim looked up as they walked. Father was smiling as Ephraim's blank face stared in stupefied shock. "The walls! They…" Ephraim looked back in the direction of the cave; now many hundreds of meters behind them.

"Yes?"

"Those walls had to be as hard as the diamonds themselves to hold them in the positions they were in!"

"Yes." Father nodded.

"The weight and shape of these diamonds! There's no way they should have been able to be supported the way they were!"

Father looked at Ephraim, allowing him to continue at his own pace.

"And then, the walls! For the walls to be able to release these diamonds while I was singing! What…I….I don't understand."

"That is not new."

Ephraim laughed.

"Oh yeah. I forgot. You're right. It's not new. I just…I just don't get it."

"Do you have to 'get it' in order to describe the diamond?"

"Well, yeah! I mean, I've always prided myself on that in the all-hands meetings! I can tell people all about the history of the rock and the density of the walls. I tell them about the metal content in the earth and the ways the gems and precious metals fit in their places and why, and…"

"It's what you've always done."

"Right! I…Oh…" Ephraim pulled up to a stop. "That's not the most important thing, is it?"

Father smiled. "No, Ephraim. It's not."

"What did I tell you when I first recruited you? I said, Ephraim, I am bringing people out of the Ice Kingdom. They need to know my mountain and join me here. Teach the mountain, Ephraim…"

"Uphill and downhill." They both said it together.

"And that's not really what the mountain's about, is it?" Ephraim asked as they started walking.

"Not usually. No." Father smiled.

"Wow. I've given so many bad presentations. Haven't I?" Ephraim looked at his feet.
"You gave the presentations you knew how to give," Father said. "Now, you can give different ones! And yes…" He smiled, "better ones."

"Wait," Ephraim paused. "Why did the light flicker just then? I was talking about my own presentation, not anything about you."

"Well, that's the thing, Ephraim." Father put his hand on Ephraim's shoulder as they looked at each other plainly. "You thought about yourself, yes. But when your thoughts turned negative, it wasn't just about you any more, Ephraim."

"It wasn't? I'm the one who gave the presentation. I'm the one who got so focused on the details that I didn't really talk about the mountain!"

"Yes, but Ephraim, I made you. You are mine."

Ephraim's partial smile showed hope and a touch of pain as

he looked at Father.

"And you are not a mistake."

Ephraim listened.

"Ephraim, there's an important difference between growing up and hating the things you were. I will always help you grow up, but I want you to stop short of hating yourself for who you were - even in the most terrible of mistakes."

"Even when I was upside down."

"Ha! Yes; that's right." Father put his other hand on Ephraim's shoulder. "When you were upside down, I loved you and provided for you. I spared you the pain of your condition. I looked out for you. I guarded you. I stopped you from getting into the normal catastrophes that accompany being upside down for any length of time."

Father continued, "I love you because of what I have done and who I am. That love hasn't changed when the things you've done have been bad."

Ephraim had no words to describe his thoughts and feelings. He turned and started walking. Father joined him. "Thank you, Father," was all he could say.

CHAPTER 10: BEYOND INFORMATION AND IGNORANCE

A few minutes passed in silence. Only the light sound of footfalls could be heard. Then, Father asked Ephraim, "So, when you give your presentation, who do you think will come?"

"Who will come? Oh, I don't know. I guess, the same old people who always come."

"Ohhh, the same old people? Eh?"

"Oh, no. Don't tell me."

"I won't."

"I need to stop thinking about them the way I thought about myself; don't I?"

"Sounds like a good plan, to me!" Father said, beaming.

"Because you love me just like you love them! You freed them from the ice just like you freed me. And! And, you love them because of who you are and who you say they are, not because of what they've done?"

"Seems like you're getting it! Anyone I've pulled from the ice, freed by my death, they are new!"

"And it doesn't matter what they do or what I do! You'll just fix it again!"

The light's crashed off. Ephraim stopped up short in his stride. "What…did…I….say?"

Silence.

"Father?"

"Yes, Ephraim."

"Was this just in me again?"

"Not this time, Ephraim."

"I'm sorry. I don't know. I just. I don't know what I did wrong."

"Ephraim, listen closely. The walls are asking to force you

out. I'm not letting them."

Force me out?

"The walls want me to insist that you go back to the elevator immediately. But I am here with you. Don't be afraid, Ephraim."

"But Father." Ephraim couldn't keep the shudder and fear out of his voice. "Did I step in a puddle or something? I don't understand what I did."

"Ephraim. I understand you are confused. You are learning, and I love you. But, Ephraim, it must never be that any one freed from the ice, believes that their decisions don't matter."

Oh no. That was it!

"That would be a complete misunderstanding of my love, but also of my essence as the whole and united Father that I am.

My ways are right. My ways are true.
My ways are higher and brighter than you.
My love is whole. My love is strong.
And I never rejoice in, or love what is wrong.
You've been forgiven, and here's what else…
You'll never be perfect without my help!
But, Ephraim, listen to what I now say:
My kindness is costly each and every day.
Wholeness, and rightness aren't just things that I seek,
They're me from my depths, to my highest peak!
So when I have people who've been set free
I want them to follow my ways; follow me!
My rules aren't a list of just do's, don'ts and shoulds!
My path is strong, sound, and firm; it's good.
So, Ephraim, please, I want you to know
It matters how you live; I want you to grow.
It makes all the difference when you choose the right
Even though I'll never send you back in the Ice-night.

I saw you there; loved you. I know all even from afar!
With my death, I made you free, and now, free you are.
So, follow me, Ephraim! Now you're thawed, free to choose!
And with my ways, you'll stay free! With my love, you can't lose!"

Ephraim was speechless for many breaths.

"Your song..." Ephraim started. "Your song was beautiful and terrible at the same time."

"Yes, Ephraim. As am I."

"I never want to get that wrong, ever again. Thank you for protecting me from the rocks. Do they hate me?"

"No, they don't hate you, Ephraim. They don't really hate or love anyone. Though, you could call it love that they have for me."

"The rocks can tell when right or wrong goes on within them; but they don't hate you. They just wanted to expel the wrong from inside them."

"That's very good. I'm glad you are more tender than they are - and patient. Thank you for teaching me and not just discarding me when I make a mistake."

"I'm the King of every Mountain, mighty and fierce! I'll show you what's right because I define what is right!"

The light around Father and Ephraim swelled to a great strength! Ephraim was convinced that light would have burned had it come from the sun. The reds burned and the orange gleamed, turning into a yellow, then a pure white light! He tried to shield his eyes, but the light was stronger than the hands that tried to block it. He realized then, that this light was stronger than the sun's. *The only reason I'm not burning is because of Father, Himself!*

"And Ephraim, I'm also the Hope of the Miner, gracious and

loving! I'll shield you from the weight of my own ferocity. I'll keep you from being crushed and help you grow and change. Ephraim, follow me and I won't keep anything good from you."

The light didn't fade while Father spoke again. Instead, the white colors cooled into yellows, oranges and reds, then into blues, greens, indigo and violets. All were strong, like a raging fire and ocean flood; but each was unique in their ways.

"Father." Ephraim sighed, bringing his hands down as the prismatic assault on his senses returned to the brightness it had maintained since they'd started walking. "Thank you." Ephraim breathed deeply. "Thank you for letting me know who You are. I'm sorry I misunderstood."

"Ephraim. I love you." Father stopped Ephraim from walking on. "But you didn't just misunderstand."

"I didn't?"

"No. To misunderstand is a matter of the mind and lacking information. Your error was in how you thought of me and what you believed. Your heart wanted to believe that your choices didn't matter."

Ephraim's eyes widened and he held his mouth slightly open. *He's right!*

"I welcome your ignorance. But I will correct you when your heart is not strong in my ways. Ignorance is emptiness, a mind that can be informed. A heart must be changed, it must be corrected and persuaded - wooed to another way, enchanted with another melody."

"Will you sing me another song?"

"Soon, Ephraim. Soon. For now, it is time for you to rest."

Ephraim looked at Father. "I don't need to rest! I'm fine! I—"

Father had led him to an open room in the mountain

where there was a spongy floor. Ephraim lowered himself down on the earth at his feet. Now, having heard the invitation, Ephraim couldn't stay awake. Ephraim had moved without thinking; sprawling out on the floor and quickly falling sound asleep. Father covered Ephraim, pulling a blanket of light from the air. It warmed him as it hovered, remaining a few inches above Ephraim as he lay - soundly sleeping.

CHAPTER 11: FROM
LEVEL TO LEVEL

Ephraim awoke with a feeling of refreshment he'd never experienced before. *I am wide awake. I was asleep and now I am completely awake!*

He stood up and the spongy ground under him seemed to inhale a bit and regained its height and fullness from the areas where Ephraim had slept. "Fath—"

"Hello Ephraim." The light of Ephraim's blanket spiraled and spooled, coiling up, then splashing into the light that constantly swirled around Father.

"Hello, Father! Is it morning?"

"In my mountain, it is always morning. There is always hope, always opportunity, always curiosity. Even in the cool of the sun's setting, and the shine of the moon's glory - it is morning wherever I am. Now, let's continue as you prepare for your presentation."

"My presentation!" Ephraim brought his hand to his forehead with a sharp "*Smack!*"

"How much time do I have?"

"It will be tomorrow."

"Tomorrow! How can that be?!" Ephraim's mouth hung open and his eyes were globes, as he looked at Father. "I won't be ready! I have so much to do, so much to research! I still have so much to understand! I don't know the history of the diamonds? What if I measured wrong? I wanted to talk about their twinkle. Even if it is a little dull. I wanted...to..."

Father was smiling and beginning to hold up his hand.

"I...thought..."

"The time you have is the time you have, Ephraim."

"Wait! Father! I almost forgot!"

Father listened.

"As I got up from the ground...were those mushrooms I laid

on?" Ephraim's thoughts seemed to trail off. Then, he recovered his focus. "Anyway, sorry. As I got up, I had a thought! For a moment, I thought about the ceiling and the floor and I'm confused."

"Go on." Father's warmth was so authentic. It was genuine, never forced. Never patronizing or insulting. His smile seemed new every time, but Ephraim's eyes saw the same greeting.

"Well, if I was upside down and I thought I was going down when I was coming to work and getting into the elevator." Ephraim was motioning with his hands and closing his eyes as he tried to mime the idea he struggled to articulate. "But you said everyone you've freed from the ice goes up from level to level. The miner's guide tells us and you said it here! You said, 'When we, with our faces freed from the ice - when we talk with you, think of you, stay near you…you move us from level to level!"

"Ahh." Father said as he listened.

"So," Ephraim shut his eyes. Making one hand into a shelf and moving it up in the air, then moving it down and bringing the other hand into a shelf and up over it. He moved them up and down, one sliding down in the air as the other moved from the bottom to the top, then slid down too. The hands overlapped as they moved. "What happened when I was going down? How is that level to level? Did you mean going down levels, too?"

"Ephraim. This is very important. I'm so glad you asked." Father nodded and smiled. He moved his hands like Ephraim had. "You did well in your explanation and how you tried to make sense of it, Ephraim."

Ephraim gave a one-sided grin. He wasn't sure how this conversation would go.

I trust Father, but I'm learning that His answers don't always feel good. Sometimes they really sting. I know they're good answers. He's good and, really, He's perfect. But that doesn't mean that His answers won't hurt. He said this was important. 'Very important!'

"Ephraim, what you feel is not always the whole truth. Your feelings represent a reality, but only a reality of what you think and sense in the moment. That's not the same as the truth of what's happening around you. As a matter of fact, what you feel is hardly ever the whole truth because only I know the whole truth. And sometimes, Ephraim, what you feel isn't at all in line with any other truth outside of you."

Here it comes. Ephraim prepared himself with an invisible wince.

"While you were upside down, you got to a place where you were always feeling horrible. You were heavy-hearted, grief-stricken, sour, and becoming bitter. You attacked the mine like a violent thief instead of a friend. You felt that I was merely your boss, commanding you what to do and where to do it."

Father looked at Ephraim to make sure he was listening.

Ephraim looked at Father, attentive to His words.

"You were upside down, and every time you finished a level, you went down lower. But—"

"But I was actually going higher!"

"But, you were actually going higher. That's correct."

"But how can that be a good thing? If I was upside down, and higher is better…and every time I got worse and worse in my frustration and discouragement, I thought I was going deeper into the caverns and lower into the mountain…but I was actually… going higher in the mountain?"

"Ephraim, where did I meet you the other day? Where did I come for you in the way that you could see?"

"In the Gold Gateway."

"Had you ever dug deeper - in your mind?"

"No, that was the lowest I'd been."

"Ephraim, it was the lowest you'd been, but you were always in my mountain. You always belonged to me."

Ephraim looked at Father carefully, hanging on every word He said.

"Ephraim, because you belonged to me, I was planning everything you experienced from the start. I know it seemed the lowest you'd ever been, but it was the only pathway to being closer to me."

Ephraim could only blink and listen.

"It's true, you were in a very bad place. If you'd been alone, it would have been fatal. If you were alone, the deeper you got, the farther away you would have been from rescue."

I didn't think about that. Ephraim mused.

"Instead, your greater pain...Ephraim." Ephraim looked at Father closely, so curious about what he would say next. "Your greater pain was the pathway for your greater growth."

The mountain creaked. Ephraim looked up at Father with concern.

"She knows this song I sing," Father said, putting his hand on the wall closest to him. "I've sung it to her for ages."

Father continued. "The mountain has been subject to the pains and aches, the picks and chisels, the mallets and carts of freed people for many, many years."

"I'm sorry I took out my frustration on the mountain," Ephraim said, looking warily at the mountain above him.

"I have told her," Father said. "Thank you Ephraim. She waits. She waits for me. One day, her frustration will be over and she will sing with me fully."

The mountain creaked again, almost seeming to moan in Ephraim's ears.

"Was that the mountain?!"

"It was," Father said. "I made her for this age, but I did not make her to stay in this age forever. She's not designed for this."

"I don't understand," Ephraim kept watch on the walls around him. They seemed to shimmer with the light in a different way.

"You will. But for now, know this thing that the mountain shares with you: your pain was the pathway for your greater growth."

Ephraim focused on Father's face again and Father spoke.

"I have a plan for the mountain, Ephraim; as I have a plan for you. When you were upside-down, I sustained you in your pain and confusion. For you - those of you whom I have made like myself - for you, even more than the mountain, I am with you. I am with you and I am for you. I love you and I understand you in your pain. What seemed like increased pain and hardship was preparing you for a rise in the levels you worked."

Father paused.

"You could not have struck gold farther down in the mountain, Ephraim."

That makes sense!

"There is no gold for you in the depths. That is a prize held only for higher levels."

Ephraim smiled, "So, while I thought and felt like I was only getting worse, I was actually growing?"

"That's right, Ephraim. Much growth is that way."

Ephraim felt hope stirring inside himself.

"Just as you did not appreciate the gold, you could not have appreciated the growth as long as you were upside-down. So, to you, it didn't feel like you were growing."

"It definitely did not!"

"I know, Ephraim. I know."

"It felt miserable!"

"Yes, I remember."

"You remember?"

"Yes, Ephraim. I was with you every moment of every day. Even though you didn't see me or want to see me, I was with you. Occasionally, I would even call for you, when it hurt me so much to see you hurting and afraid."

"You called for me? When?"

"The last time was just recently, when you were in the darkness! I hated seeing you so afraid. I called for you, but you could not understand."

"Father, I'm sorry."

"Eeepppphraiiimm!" Father cupped his hand and called for Ephraim.

"Wait! Do that again?!"

"Eeeeeepppphhhhhraiiiim!"

"That was you!"

"Yes, child. I called for you every day. Sometimes multiple times a day!"

"Oh Father. I heard you. I heard you and I ignored you."

"I saw you, Ephraim. I saw you look up and then go back to work without even acknowledging me. The pain of seeing my child ignore my voice was so terrible."

"Father, I'm afraid it is worse than that. I didn't just ignore it."

"Tell me," Father motioned him on.

"Father, I heard your voice; not as an appeal or invitation to come to you." Ephraim hung his head. His forehead almost touched the diamonds in his hands as he stood still, full of emotion. "Father, I heard your voice...as a call...to work harder." Ephraim shook with emotion. "I thought...I thought that was a call from the camp. I thought it was a shift alarm, reminding us to get to work in our mines." Ephraim tossed down the diamonds and flung his arms around his Father.

"I know you did, Ephraim. I know."

The two stood in their embrace as the lights flowing around Father coursed between them and around them in flourishes of green and occasional ribbons of amber, slowly morphing into the familiar waves again.

"How can I make sure I never get to that point again?!" Ephraim emerged from Father's chest with angst, as he clung to him.

"Follow me, Ephraim. Stay with me, talk with me, walk with me. Follow me."

"I want to, Father."

"I want you to, Ephraim."

"Right now, though..." Father pulled away from Ephraim, "we have work to do."

"Father, do I have to?" Father motioned to the floor where

the diamonds lay.

"The time you have is the time you have. No more, no less."

"I know, Father, but all my presentations before have been so well thought out and so composed!"

"Have they?"

"How can I do that in the time I have left, today?" Ephraim bent down to pick up the diamonds.

"Who said that I wanted your presentation tomorrow to be like anything you've done before?"

CHAPTER 12: TREASURE DEFINED

Ephraim looked at the diamonds. He wondered what he could say about them.

"Father, I don't know how to talk about these."

"Yes, you do, Ephraim."

Father picked one up and tossed it in the air. Ephraim could only watch in awe.

"It responds to you!"

"Doesn't it!" Father smiled as the huge gem spun, end over end, twisting and tilting in a manner more like a ballerina's pirouette than a chunk of rock from a wall.

"Ephraim, you've already described the diamond to me. You've understood its origins well. You've even seen it in my hands!"

"Yes?"

"So, Ephraim, rest. You have that information in your mind and you know what to say about it."

"Okay..." Ephraim looked at Father, confused. "So, that's all? I guess I do know that. Thank you, Father. I just—"

"Oh no; that's not all." Father smiled and spread his arms wide.

"It's not? But I thought that's what it meant to teach the gems...'uphill and downhill.'"

"No, Ephraim," Father shook his head while he grinned. "That's what I said, but that's not what it means."

Father turned to Ephraim. "Ephraim, do you love gold?" Father reached up to the mountain, touched it and there was a spark that brightened everything around them! As Ephraim watched, the spark ran all around and through the walls, like a bolt of lightning but slow; slow enough so Ephraim could watch the path as it ran through the stone. Ephraim's mouth hung open. He had begun to point at the bright bead of light that ran ahead in front of the line light in the rock.

"Is that..." He looked at Father. "Is that gold?"

"It is!"

"You just...Did you just make gold in this stone we're standing in?"

"Would you like some?"

"Yes, please."

A place where the light had split off into a separate vein of gold suddenly brightened. It swelled momentarily, pulsing with light. Then it fell out of the wall as a rope, where it hung from one side, in the midst of the rock where they stood. It was glowing.

"Do I...just..." Ephraim looked at Father.

"Yes, take it!" Father laughed as Ephraim reached out and took the shimmering rope of gold. It moved in his hands like a two-inch thick braid of a hundred thousand threads of the shining metal.

Ephraim had maneuvered the diamonds into one hand. He stared at the rope and then put it over his shoulder.

"Is this how all gold looks in the walls?"

"When it's young," said Father.

Ephraim adjusted the large diamonds in his hands again. "Here," Father said as he nodded to the rope. The two ends joined so the rope made a sort of large necklace, without clasp or seams, on Ephraim's shoulders.

"Ephraim," Father began walking again, but turned to Ephraim as he walked.

"Yes?"

"Do you love gold?"

"I love it! Thank you so much! I will always cherish this gift, Father!"

"Ephraim, would you love this braid if it were made of wood?"

"Wood?" Ephraim bent his head to try and look down at the necklace. "I don't know."

"Well...will you spend this necklace? Gold is very valuable!"

"Oh, no. Never! How could I spend it?! I will always keep this in my home. I will never forget seeing you touch the mountain and watching the gold appear!"

"So, what makes it a treasure?"

"Well...I guess..." Ephraim slowed his walking pace.

"If you're not going to spend it, what makes it a treasure?" Father asked again. "Take your time," Father said. Then He walked on. Ephraim kept pace, but all of his other movements had slowed down as he pondered Father's question.

"Here!" Father laughed. "I'll help you!"

"What do you me—" Suddenly, the rope around Ephraim's neck disappeared. "Wha—?!" Ephraim jumbled the diamonds in his panic. "No! It..." Ephraim got the diamonds situated and grabbed for his golden necklace. Sure enough, it was there when he reached for it. As he held it up though, Ephraim realized why he'd thought it was gone.

Instead of a weighty rope of golden thread, two inches thick - Ephraim found something different. "Is this wood?" He asked, but Father was far ahead now.

"Take your time!" Father called back. "Catch up when you're ready!"

It was wood. Ephraim's beautiful necklace had turned from shimmering gold, poured from the mountain, to this wooden... thing. *What did I do to have this happen? I don't understand. We've had such a good time together. And now Father has taken back the gold?*

Ephraim hunched his shoulders and started to walk again.

After five or six steps, though, Ephraim stopped.

Wait a second! Look at me! I'm still walking in a mountain! I'm in the rock! What am I even walking on? I'm walking on some sort of ground even though I'm in the mountain itself!

Oh! Ha! And I'd better not start getting down on myself or about Father since He's up there. I don't want the mountain to spit me out, like it wanted to before!

"Sorry rock! Sorry mountain!" Ephraim raised his eyes to the walls around him. He ducked for a few paces as if the walls would fall on him.

So, what am I doing here? What does Father want me to

understand? He's not mad at me. If He were mad at me, He would tell me. And if He were mad at me, Father wouldn't be up there. He doesn't abandon me when He's upset, He corrects me. Even if it stings.

Ephraim winced.

So, we're still together, it's just that Father wants me to think about something. He said to 'Catch up' when I'm ready. Oh, right! And He asked me what makes this necklace a treasure...well, when it was gold. He said, 'What makes it a treasure if you're not going to spend it?' Sheesh. I don't know. It's special for a lot of reasons! I dug for gold last week! Then, I dug for gold a few days ago! I thought I was going to find gold again! That made this gold special.

Well...not really. I don't even think of this gold like that. Why not? Oh, that's a question like Father asks. Ha!

Why don't I think of this gold like the gold I was searching for before? Sheesh, well, so much has changed. Look where I am! I'm in the mountain! That's changed! I'm seeing all these colors around me! That's changed!

I'm not upside-down anymore! That's changed! Look how I acted when I didn't find gold! That's changed! I was so angry and confused. I was just so down on myself! That's so...
Ephraim grimaced, and then calmed his face.

Wait, slow down. I don't need to put myself down for that. What did Father say? The past is past and now I have a chance to create a new past...right now! But that's changed! I see my job differently! I was bitter before and now I'm not! I was afraid before and now, I'm not! Before, I was...I thought I was alone.

Ephraim walked in silence for a moment.
Hello Father. He thought.

"Hello Ephraim." Ephraim heard Father's voice in his thoughts.

Ephraim smiled. *And now, I'm not alone. I know it now. But even my thoughts about the treasures have changed! I'm carrying these ugly diamonds now! That's changed!*

His eyes widened. *Uhh. Yeah. Hello Father.*
"Hello Ephraim."
I'm sorry I thought the diamonds were ugly.
"I know you did, Ephraim."
And I forgot that you know my heart even if I don't say it.
"I forgive you, Ephraim."
So, I'm not upside-down! I'm walking through the mountains.
I've sung the songs with Father. I have seen all these lights because...
Wait! That's it! That's the biggest thing that's changed!
"Yes." Father affirmed him.
Father! I'm walking and talking with Father again!

Ephraim beamed. He tucked the diamonds into his chest and started off running!

As he ran, he began to sing!

"Father! Oh my Father! You've changed my everything!
You've given me my freedom from the ice and now I sing!
You've brought me to your mountain; here,
we walk and talk all day!
You've taught me that I'm not alone! When I'm stuck, I'll say...

Father, I'm so thankful!
With you, I'm now so free!
You've rescued me from empty work
And from my misery!

Father! This is your mountain!
Your hill's my joy I see!
It's the place where I'm with you!
And where you are, I want to be!"

Just as Ephraim caught up to Father, Father turned to him with the most playful look Ephraim could imagine!

"Ephraim...let's ruuuuun!"

In anyone else, I'd say Father looked sneaky! But there's nothing sneaky about Him!

Father began to sing Ephraim's song back to him and that made Ephraim overjoyed! *He knows my song! The song I just made up!*

"Where do you think the good things come from in you?"

From You! Of course!

The two of them ran on. Ephraim laughed as he ran.

They ran up into the mountain, through caves and through pools of shining water!

*Ohhh, water....*Ephraim laughed to himself, remembering hearing water when he was afraid.

They ran down through the levels, too! Then, they kept running down farther and farther. Soon, Ephraim noticed the levels he'd worked through the years.

Topaz! Agate! Turquoise! Emerald! Ruby! Garnet! Ha! Limestone! "I love you, limestone! Now that my Father is with me!" Ephraim called out as he ran through each level with Father.

Ephraim noticed they were not slowing down. *We're going so fast. So fast and I don't feel it at all! It's amazing! But...shouldn't we be slowing down? We're coming to the bottom!*

"Are we?!" Father's voice called out as they ran.

What does that mean?!

Father ran ahead. Ephraim caught up.

Father ran ahead more, laughing! Ephraim caught up, laughing!

The two ran down and down, past the main level. Now, they were hundreds of meters below the ground level. "Father, what is below your mountain?"

"Oh, there's no such thing, Ephraim."

"No such thing?"

"No, it's all my mountain. Even the towns where ice holds people prisoner."

Ephraim could only listen.

"That's why it hurts so much. My people and my mountain are everywhere. And my people are held captive."

Ephraim looked sad.

"Thank you for grieving with me, Ephraim."

Father continued, "But that's not why we're here. Ephraim, you were not going down into the rock below..."

"Yes, Father, I remember."

"Ephraim, you will never mine these treasures."

Father pointed. In the distance, farther below even from where they had stopped, Ephraim could see what looked like great pools of shimmering oceans of light.

"Oh, ok, Father. I understand."

"You do not."

"Ok. Father. I don't understand."

"Well said," Father smiled. "Ephraim, only I will bring these up. And it will be a day not far from now. But it is not yet."

"Oh, Father! You will bring up these...these...lakes? What are they? Water? The cleanest water anyone has ever heard of?"

"No, Ephraim. I will only speak a little about these, for now. These are but pools of precious jewels, still to be formed."

Father closed his eyes.

He continued. "These are the pools I will one day bring forth into mountains of their own. Very treasured mountains. Treasured…" Father looked at Ephraim and winked. "Treasured because I will be with you and I will bring these with me. Jasper, gold, clear as glass. Look, lakes of pearl!"

I thought…that pearl…

"Not all things must be created the same way every time, Ephraim." He smiled. "There are no shells big enough for the plans I have with this pearl." Father pointed in the distance. "Look at the pools of beryl, chrysolite, onyx, carnelian, emerald, agate, sapphire, topaz, chrysoprase, and jacinth! Amethyst! And so many more!"

Ephraim could only look in wonder as the expansive lakes of jewels seemed to hover in the earth in front of him for miles. Even from so far away, they shimmered and danced in the light, reflecting from Father as he stood with Ephraim.

"Now! Let's go up!"

"Ok!"

The two ran back up through the mountain.

"Oh, Father!" Ephraim called.

"Yes, Ephraim."

"Thank you for showing me those lakes and pools. The jewels were majestic!"

"I'm glad you enjoyed them. Do not say much about them for now. You will see them one day."

"Ok, Father!" Ephraim wondered about that statement from Father. "But also, Father! I understand what makes this necklace a treasure to me. Whether you leave it as wood or turn it to gold."

"Yes, Ephraim?"

"It's You, Father." Suddenly, Ephraim felt the weight on his neck again. The rope was gold, yet again. "You have changed everything! Because of You, Father, this necklace is my prize. Not because it is gold. Because of You, my whole life has been changed, Father. The gold necklace, the diamonds, the mountain."

Ephraim inhaled. "Father! Everything is better because of You! Everything has meaning now, because I'm seeing it with You and through You I see everything!"

Father glowed for Ephraim to see.

Then, he glowed brighter; and laughed with joy!

Ephraim laughed with Father.

Then, Father glowed brighter! And Ephraim squinted.

"Show them! Ephraim. Show them. Tell them of the treasure and where it gets its worth!"

"I will!" Ephraim called, holding his hands up to the light. "I will with Your help!"

CHAPTER 13: THE HEART OF THE MOUNTAIN

Suddenly, Ephraim and Father emerged from the mountain. They stood on the firm ground like every other day. No walking through rocks or breathing in the midst of stone.

In his hands, Ephraim could feel the two diamonds. Without even looking, his hands knew what to do as he packed them into his bag. Then, he moved to tuck in the necklace, awkwardly pushing it under his collar.

"Remember, Ephraim."

Ephraim turned to Father, then flinched. "Foreman?!"

"Don't be afraid, Ephraim. You know me. It's just that not everyone is ready to see me as you did in the mountain."

Father, who was Foreman, patted Ephraim on the shoulders.

"I'll see you at the meeting tomorrow!" He smiled, turned, and walked away.

"Hey, Preacher!" A voice called over Ephraim's shoulder. "Hey Preacher! You gonna stand there all day? I gotta get my gems filed and put away! You're not the only one with an all-hands meeting tomorrow!"

"Oh!" Ephraim pulled up and stepped out of the way as his coworker, Musician, shuffled past him. "Sorry!" Ephraim said. "And..." Musician moved on, humming. Quickly, he was out of earshot as Ephraim said, "and, it's Ephraim." Ephraim's face fell a little as he wondered what he should do. His thoughts swirled.

Some day, we'll talk more. Today, I have to focus, and do my part.

Ephraim walked to his car, got in, and drove away from the mountain and the mobile buildings around it. Looking in his rearview mirror, Ephraim thought about all he'd done this week in the mountain, with Father.

The next morning, Ephraim woke up early. He kissed his wife and made breakfast for everyone.

"Aren't you going to be late for the all-hands meeting?" She asked, returning his kiss.

"Nope. It will be fine." Ephraim said.

"Well, Preacher, you usually have to get to the meeting so early!"

"I know. Today, though, I'm making breakfast for my family. I'll go in a minute," Ephraim said. "And honey..." She turned to look at him. "Call me Ephraim again, okay?"

Ephraim's wife smiled broadly. "I never stopped in my heart!"

The family sat through breakfast, laughing and enjoying dad's pancakes. Then, he said, "Well, I'd better get going! I'll see you all soon!"

"Bye, Daddy!" "Bye Dad!" "See ya, Pop!" "Goodbye, dear. I'll see you soon!"

Ephraim drove off through town. As he drove, he smiled and sang to himself. Ephraim was so grateful to have a relationship with Father the way he did!

Then, Ephraim came to the four-way stop.

Ephraim got out.

He held up his hands, and cried. "Father! I love you! I thank you for loving me! Thank you that you are always with me! Thank you that I am never al—"

"Never alone."

"Hello Father!"

"Hello Ephraim. Let's get in."

The two got in the car and Ephraim drove on.

"Do you know what you'll say?"

"I do, Father."

"Ephraim, what I've done here, I did for you."

Ephraim was shocked to look around and see that he and Father were in the mountain again.

"You may tell everyone about the gems and precious metals because that is the language I want you to use."

"Okay, Father."

"But Ephraim, never forget. You search the mines and find the gems, metals, and precious stones. And you think that in them you have all you need! But these gems, they point to me! They are always meant to point to me so you can have true life and never be alone."

"Ephraim, what is the beauty of the gems but your relationship with me?"

And then, in a blink, Ephraim found himself speaking to the all-hands meeting. Smoothly, he spoke like nothing special had happened. Ephraim looked around and saw the modest crowd. He thought of how each of the listeners was special to Father. Now, they were more special to him, as well.

"These" he smiled, "are the dimensions of the diamonds! They are 12" by 7" and their cut is..." Ephraim pulled the diamonds out from his pack and set them on the pulpit in front of him.

Gasps filled the air! Murmurs bubbled up from all around the meeting room.

"These gems that I've described for you..." Ephraim pointed to the dull diamonds he'd seen in the mountains. The diamonds he'd carried home and back to the meeting. "These are...well, they're kind of beautiful, it's true." Ephraim knew the people would have a hard time appreciating his words about the diamonds being beautiful. He knew there would be someone who would call him a fraud. Some would accuse him of misleading them. Someone would try to tell Ephraim that he was confused; that there was no way these could actually be diamonds. Still, Ephraim continued.

"But even with these diamonds, they are only treasures because of the Father!" Ephraim noticed Foreman in the corner of the room as he spoke. He gave a wince, but Foreman nodded him on. *He knows I need the help. These people are going to rip me to shreds. They'll hate this presentation! Cloudy diamonds and a preacher who can't think straight.*

"Friends! The Father wants a relationship with each of us! The gems are the means by which he's inviting us to His mountain! Not so that everyone gets caught up in the gems, but so that we'll all walk with Him, talk with Him, and discover what it is like to know Him forever!"

CHAPTER 14: LOW LIGHTS AND VISION: STRANGELY DIMMED

"I don't need miners, Ephraim."

The meeting had ended and Ephraim was walking with Father through the first level of the mountain.

"That's good because I don't know what happened in there! Everyone is blind!"

Father looked at Ephraim.

"I finished talking and they stormed the stage at the end!"

"All they could talk about was this!" Ephraim pulled one of the diamonds out and turned it over in his hands. "They couldn't stop asking me about mining! They begged me to tell them where to dig and how to pick the best tools. They said I had to tell them!" Ephraim looked at Father with sadness.

"They didn't even ask about my time with You!" Ephraim held his head low.

"They just asked about maps, axes, chisels and diamonds!"

"Ephraim," Father beckoned.

"I'm sorry, Father, I failed You. I thought I'd do better. I really did enjoy my time with You. So much!"

"Ephraim, you did everything I wanted you to do."

"How could that be?"

"Ephraim, your priority was to be with me. To walk with me, and talk with me." Father turned and took the diamond from Ephraim's hands.

Ephraim was happy to give it back.

I don't know what to do with that now.

"Ephraim, I'm going to take you back to where I found you last week. I want to show you something."

Don't be afraid. Father loves you. Don't be afraid.

"Look around, Ephraim."

Ephraim looked around where he stood with Father.

"Don't be alarmed, Ephraim. I'm going to let you see me as Foreman again."

Ok, that's not so—

"Only Foreman, Ephraim."

"Wait, no!"

The lights blinked out. No waves of color. No lights at all. No songs hung in the air.

"Teetle clup…Blupp."

Don't panic. Don't panic. Father. I know I'm not alone.

"You are not alone."

"Thank you, Father."

Suddenly, Ephraim saw the lamp from his hard hat. It turned on and moved around a little in the air. Then, Father handed it to Ephraim. "Put this on."

Ephraim put on the hard hat.

To see Foreman in the light of the lamp was jarring for Ephraim.

"Father…I—"

"It will not be like this for long, Ephraim. Only just for a moment."

"Okay, Father. I trust You."

"Yes, you do, now. Ephraim."

Father reached into his vest pocket and pulled out something large.

"Whaaa!" As soon as the lamplight fell on the gemstone, Ephraim winced and turned away.

"No, Ephraim. Look at it closely."

Ephraim turned back to the gem. The colors it radiated were beautiful! Ephraim was in shock. He naturally held out his hands and reached for it without thinking. "Can...can I hold it?"

"Of course you can. It's yours!" Foreman put the gem into Ephraim's hands.

"My—" Ephraim was shocked. "Mine?! How could..." Suddenly, Ephraim had a flood of recognition. "My diamond!" He held it up in the cavern and pointed the lamp fully onto the diamond. "It shines!"

Foreman smiled and only looked at Ephraim as realization overtook him, leading to appreciation. "Yes, Ephraim." Foreman's smile was not full, like Father's.

"Is..." Ephraim looked at Foreman. "Is this how it really looks? Why couldn't I see this when I looked at it before? Did something happen to my eyes?"

"Ephraim…"

"Is this what everyone else saw at the meeting?! No wonder they were amazed and wanted to know more!"

"Yes, Ephraim. This is what many of them saw."

"But…how? Why?"

"Ephraim, for those who have never seen me as Father, this is the brightest thing they can imagine. This diamond is radiant for them."

Ephraim looked with the lamp shining fully on Foreman's face.

"Their eyes are like yours were, Ephraim. Even now, many of those who heard your presentation are going around talking together or telling their friends and family about the diamond. They're talking about you, Ephraim."

"Oh no!"

"It's not the worst thing. Some of them are talking about me. But even many of those who talk about you are doing so because they can't even imagine seeing me as you have."

Father immediately changed from Foreman to the light emitting, radiant Father Ephraim knew and loved. "There you are!" Ephraim jumped to embrace his Father.

When he did, the lamp light on his head fell off and the grey light it emitted blinked out again as it hit the ceiling.

"Many of them will talk of you, Ephraim. Some will want to learn from you. And you must lead them to me."

"Oh, I will!" Ephraim renewed the embrace of Father. "I will, I will!"

"I know. And I will help you."

"I don't want them to think of me! I want them to think of You! I want them to become miners and follow You and walk with You and talk with You, Father!"

"Yes, Ephraim. And you will."

Father let Ephraim wear himself out in his embrace.

When they pulled away from each other, Father walked with Ephraim toward the entrance.

As they walked, Father spread his fingers and lightly pulled them through the stone and rock all around them. In the path of each finger, there erupted tiny rivers of shining colors.

"What are those?"

"Watch!" They cooled into turquoise, onyx. ruby, gold, and amethyst. "Why should the telling possibly be as good as the living, Ephraim? How could it ever be?"

Ephraim just watched the precious stones and gems cool from their liquid states.

"Ephraim, to present and mine is to be a little frustrated."
"What do you mean?"

"You will always walk and talk with me. And when you do, you will want to share that with others! Some will want to hear of me, and some will only want the treasures you share that will benefit them outside the mountain."

Ephraim listened.

"Don't be sad about that. Just do your best with me in your heart."

"I will, with Your help, Father."

"When we are together, I will show you wonders in my mountain and in my heart, Ephraim."

"Thank You!"

"And when you are with them, show them the treasures and point them to me."

"I will. Help me to do that, Father."

"I certainly will."

The two smiled. Ephraim was rapt in wonder at all he had experienced. Father, clearly full of joy in himself and in Ephraim, His friend.

"Now, Ephraim, there is someone I want you to meet." The two walked to the mobile office. Ephraim saw a young man ahead, seated in a chair outside the office. "Ephraim, this is Will" "Will, this is Ephraim."

"Hello Will!"

"Hi."

"I'd like you to show Will around a bit, Ephraim."

"Gladly!"

Foreman walked away, leaving the two together.

"He's forgotten my name three times already!"

"Oh? Really?" Ephraim asked. "What's your name?"

"It's Protege, not Will," Will said, sheepishly. He rolled his eyes. "And everyone here calls you, Mentor"

"Oh really?!" Ephraim laughed to himself.

"Well, you can call me Ephraim."

As Ephraim started walking with his new friend, he smiled as they got in the elevator. "Ok!" Ephraim said as he closed the door behind them both. "Tell me about your drive in to work! Do you pass any four way stops?"

The End

ACKNOWLEDGEMENTS

So much life unfolds in the process of writing, rewriting, editing, and shaping a book. Through it all, my family gave me the space to laugh, weep, and sing—what a joy and gift that has been. I'm deeply grateful.

Many others have journeyed with me along the way. To the reviewers, editors, encouragers, question-askers, and grammar-minded friends: thank you. Your insights, challenges, and cheers have meant more than I can say.

To SW, EH, JH, JC, JS, HS, LB, RM, CH, BC, GS, DD, NC, MC, JC, BH, SE, KM, JH, WH, ZB and so many others: your support and encouragement have been a steady source of strength.

As a pastor, I've had the privilege of serving with and leading some truly wonderful people. Thank you for journeying with me and for celebrating the gems we uncovered together. Your hunger for the Maker of the mountain has made you a treasured companion.

To Father: thank you for the run of a lifetime, I delight in you more than all the gems in the mountain!

YOU'RE INVITED

Let's Create Together

Preacher's Tale began as a personal journey—an offering to encourage and uplift Christian workers, especially pastors and leaders. With the generous help of editors and proofreaders, it quickly grew into something richer. Now, I believe it can become something even more: a collaborative work of beauty and worship.

For this first edition, I wrote every word myself (with editorial support from friends). The images and illustrations were created using digital tools—including AI-generated images I adjusted and refined until I was pleased. Still, I long to see a future edition illustrated by human hands, overflowing from hearts that are alive and engaged with the true Hero of the story.

Imagine the miner's journey rendered in pencil, paint, or ink. Imagine the songs brought to life with original compositions and instrumentation. I would be deeply honored to include artwork and music created by those who resonate with this story, its longings, its call to faithfulness, and its rediscovery of joy in the Lord.

If you're a visual artist or a composer inspired by *Preacher's Tale*, I invite you to submit your work. Whether it's a piece of visual art based on a scene or a musical setting of one of the book's songs, I would love to consider your contribution for a future illustrated edition and companion album. Consider drawing your favorite leader or a preacher from Christian history. Maybe you sketch your pastor as Ephraim, worshiping in the fields or Preacher digging for gems? Let your creativity soar!

Please send your creations to play @ aperturework.com or tag them on Instagram using **#PreachersTaleArt** or **#PreachersTaleMusic**.

Let's make something beautiful together—a body of work that invites weary hearts to peace, to joy, to wonder, and to vital relationship with the One who walks with us through heights and depths.

With gratitude,